BAIS KAILA
TORAH PREPARATORY
HIGH SCHOOL FOR GIRLS

proudly presents
this fascinating volume
to its many friends
and supporters

Our New Lakewood Campus

Located in the world famous Torah community of Lakewood,
New Jersey, Bais Kaila High School provides the ultimate in
Torah-oriented education for girls. Bais Kaila girls are
motivated and encouraged to reach their full potential
intellectually and spiritually, with particular emphasis
on good *midos* and solid ethical and moral values.

**To receive additional copies of this book or to
have a friend included in our future mailings please write to:**

BAIS KAILA HIGH SCHOOL
Spruce and Vine Streets, P.O.B. 952, Lakewood, New Jersey 08701

*More information about the background and educational programs
of Bais Kaila High School appears at the back of the book.*

About Bais Kaila

JUST A SHORT DRIVE SOUTH OF NEW YORK CITY LIES the Torah community of Lakewood, New Jersey. Far removed from the profligate influences of the city, the tree-lined streets of this serene and picturesque town reverberate with the sweet sounds of Torah, not the clamor and blare of urban congestion. In this beautiful setting, the students of Bais Kaila High School are taught Torah and traditional values of our precious heritage. In this environment, they can truly grow into the kind of Bnos Yisroel that have always been the backbone of our people.

Bais Kaila High School was founded in 1977 by Rabbi Yisroel Schenkolewski and Rabbi Shmuel Mayer, both alumni of the world famous Lakewood Yeshiva, to serve Lakewood and the other Central Jersey communities. Over the years, the school has developed a singular blend of high caliber educational programs, both in Limudei Kodesh and secular studies, and careful attention to the individual needs of each girl. The staff is talented and experienced, and class sizes are limited to ensure warm and productive teacher-pupil relationships. At Bais Kaila, each girl is motivated and encouraged to reach her full potential, intellectually, spiritually, emotionally and socially, with particular emphasis on good *midos* and solid ethical and moral values.

The future of Bais Kaila High School is bright and full of promise. Over the past few years, our enrollment has grown very rapidly, so that we are continuously expanding our facilities. Furthermore, the already outstanding curriculum is constantly reviewed and innovative refinements added. Indeed, the philosophy of a Bais Kaila education and its implementation place the school among the foremost educational institutions of its kind.

SCAPEGOAT ON TRIAL

THE STORY OF

MENDEL BEILIS

the autobiograpy of
MENDEL BEILIS
the defendant in the notorious 1912 blood libel in Kiev

introduced and edited by
SHARI SCHWARTZ

including "The Jewish Response" by
SORA F. BULKA

cis

P·U·B·L·I·S·H·E·R·S

New York · London · Jerusalem

Copy of original 1925 edition
courtesy of the Perlow family.

Published and distributed
in the U.S., Canada and overseas by
C.I.S. Publishers and Distributors
180 Park Avenue, Lakewood, New Jersey 08701
(908) 905-3000 Fax: (908) 367-6666

Distributed in Israel by
C.I.S. International (Israel)
Rechov Mishkalov 18
Har Nof, Jerusalem
Tel: 02-518-935

Distributed in the U.K. and Europe by
C.I.S. International (U.K.)
89 Craven Park Road
London N15 6AH, England
Tel: 81-809-3723

Book and cover design: Deenee Cohen
Pictorial section: Chaya Bleier
Typography: Chaya Bleier, Nechamie Miller
Cover illustration: Maureen Scullin

ISBN 1-56062-166-4 hard cover
1-56062-167-2 soft cover

PRINTED IN THE UNITED STATES OF AMERICA

Table of Contents

Editor's Preface: The Making of a Martyr 7

War and Peace 29
A Boy Is Murdered 33
Arrested at Dawn 39
The Secret Police 43
Strange Questions 49
Behind Bars 55
The Bloody Analysis 62
The Spies 66
A Taste of Prison Life 71
My Attorneys Appear 76
A Convict with a Heart 81
New Intrigues 85
Between Hope and Despair 95
More Interrogations 102

Attorneys under Attack 106
The Attempt to Poison Me 112
A Murderer's Suicide 116
The New Indictment 119
The Trial at Last 135
Karabchevsky 140
The Trial Begins 145
Diverse Witnesses 150
More Surprises 163
Slander and Lies 169
The Tzaddikim 173
More Lies Exposed 181
The Scene of the Crime 188
The Verbal Battle 194
A Narrow Escape 201
A Verdict at Last 204
My Prison Transformed 211
Home at Last 215
A Rejoicing World 223
Provisions for the Future 229
To Palestine 233
From Kiev to Trieste 237
In the Land of Israel 242

Editor's Note: Postscript 249
Appendix: The Jewish Response 253
Pictorial Section 261

The Making of a Martyr

Mendel Beilis was a quiet, unassuming man who was to become the archetypical scapegoat, a tragic, though heroic victim whose fate epitomized the persecuted Jew in Czarist Russia. Caught up in a chain of events over which he had no control and charged with a crime of which he had no knowledge, he humbly yet bravely persevered. Forced to endure an imprisonment that included torture and solitary confinement, he finally stood trial as the whole world watched.

In his autobiography, Mendel Beilis speaks to us from a vantage point few others have experienced, much less recorded. Even though the original version of his self-published book is an awkwardly written English translation of his Yiddish manuscript, a simple eloquence shone through. It is this pathos, a poignancy that flowed from his own pen that has been so carefully preserved in this newly revised edition. Additionally, footnotes have been inserted to enhance the reader's understanding of terminology and events.

I would like to note my personal appreciation to C.I.S. Publishers for allowing me to work on a book such as this. As a historian, I welcome the opportunity to contribute to this generation's knowledge of its past; as a writer, I can think of few projects more exciting than the autobiography of an important historical figure. Anti-Semitism, Jewish persecution and the Jew as scapegoat are age-old topics that, unfortunately, are still relevant in our day.

Much has been written about Mendel Beilis, the blood libel and Russian anti-Semitism. For those interested in a more detailed study, I would recommend *The Russian Jew under Tsars and Soviets* by Salo W. Baron, *History of the Jews in Russia and Poland* by S. M. Dubnow and *The Decay of Czarism: The Beilis Trial* by Alexander B. Tager. This preface, by nature of its brevity, can only deal with these complex subjects in the most general manner. Still, we feel it is important to give this brief synopsis to allow the reader a basic orientation before he begins to read the actual words written by Mendel Beilis three-quarters of a century ago.

When I first showed the Beilis manuscript to one of my daughters, she reacted in a way that should not have surprised me. "Can it be true that Jews were really accused of killing Christian children and using their blood?" she asked incredulously. "How can such a thing be? Why did they do that?"

Why, indeed?

The answer to that question penetrates to the heart of the relationship that has existed for centuries between Jew and gentile. Tragically, much of the misery inflicted on European Jewry happened as a consequence of the terrible, macabre lie of the "blood libel," even in modern times. Yet most people instinctively associate the blood libel with a hazy medieval past and fail to realize the role this aspersion continues to play in negatively defining the Jew in the hearts and minds of the non-Jewish world.

The Blood Libel

In 1911, in Kiev, Russia, Menachem Mendel Beilis was accused of murdering a Christian child as part of a mystical religious rite and using his blood to bake Passover *matzos*. This was but the latest in a seemingly endless list of similar accusations that has plagued the Jewish people for a thousand years.

Ironically, the precursor of the blood libel was not directed at the Jews but at the early Christians. At the time, the Christians were a breakaway Jewish sect whose rapid growth was threatening the stability of the Roman Empire. Christian theology was so filled with anthropomorphic references and rites that the Romans accused the early Christians of murdering their own children in order to use their blood for ritual purposes. This charge swept through the Roman Empire and gained widespread credibility among the citizenry. After their own conversion to Christianity, the blood accusation lay dormant for centuries, but when the European Christian societies sought to oppress the Jews, who were flourishing and prospering in their midst, the accusation was resuscitated, embellished and directed at the Jewish people. Since the Jews were blamed for murdering the

9

Christian savior, whose last meal before his crucifixion had been the Passover *seder*, the allegation contended that every Passover the Jews re-enacted this crucifixion with yet another innocent Christian victim. The original victims of the accusation had become the accusers of a new victim.

The first recorded case of what was to become known as the "blood libel" can be found in the chronicles of English history. In 1144, the Jews of Norwich were officially charged with abducting, torturing and murdering a Christian child in order to use his blood for Passover. Just two years later, reports of this incident spread rapidly among the knights and peasants massing in France for the start of the Second Crusade.

One of the first eruptions of violence was in the French city of Blois. The town's Jews were dragged to a wooden tower where they were given the option of baptism or death. None chose the former. On May 26, 1171, thirty-four men and sixteen women met a fiery death in the Rhineland, with the song *Aleinu* on their lips. As if sensing the potential power of this new vehicle for further inflaming an already hostile citizenry, Rabbi Yaakov Tam, known as Rabbeinu Tam, declared the anniversary of their martyrdom a fast day in the communities of France, England and the Rhineland.

In 1181, in Vienna, Austria, upon the sworn testimony of several witnesses, the Jews were found guilty of slaughtering three Christian boys who were last seen playing on a frozen river. For this crime, three hundred Jews were burned at the stake. In the spring, the thawed river yielded the drowned, yet unharmed bodies of the three boys.

More blood libels were to follow, some attracting more

attention than others. In 1199, and in 1235, in places such as Erfurt and Lauda, in Bischofsheim and Fulda, there were more Christian accusations and more Jewish deaths.

In 1255, all the Jews of Lincoln, England, gathered for a wedding. The next day, the body of a boy named Hugh, who had been missing for a month, was found. He had probably drowned in a cesspool, but the Jews were accused of abducting him, hiding him for a month and fattening him up. It was charged that the wedding party was really a celebration of Hugh's crucifixion and that everyone had partaken of his blood. Nineteen Jews were hung without benefit of a trial.

More blood libels followed in London and Gloucester. By a decree signed on *Tishah b'Av*, July 18, 1290, all Jews were banished from England, not to be legally readmitted until the middle of the nineteenth century. Even in their absence, however, the blood libel accusation was perpetuated and the deleterious image of the Jew reinforced. A century after the banishment of the Jews of England, Chaucer wrote *The Prioress' Tale*, which centered around "Jew demons" who were handmaidens of the devil and murdered Christian children.

The enemies of the Jews promulgated these false accusations for a variety of reasons, whether as a solution for an unsolved murder or to create an opportunity for the confiscation of Jewish property or to divert the attention of a restless populace from the injustices of their own societies. And by and large, the validity of the blood libel went unquestioned, even if a particular accusation was disproved. Perhaps this particular Jew had been found innocent, but there was no doubt that the Jews and their religion still bore the guilt of the blood libel.

As the charges flourished, so did the accompanying literature, further validating the authenticity of these attacks. One
theory, published by a Dominican monk in 1263, purported the
Jews would have to commit this crime on a yearly basis, because
as a punishment for having shed the blood of the Christian
savior, they were afflicted with a terrible disease that could only
be treated with innocent Christian blood. The ritual lie and the
portrayal of the Jew as a bloodthirsty demon to be hated and
feared had become an accepted part of Christian dogma. Holy
shrines were erected to honor innocent Christian victims, and
well into the twentieth century, churches throughout Europe
displayed knives and other instruments that Jews purportedly
used for these rituals. Caricatures of hunchbacked Jews with
horns and fangs were depicted in works of art and carved into
stone decorating bridges. Proclaimed by parish priests to be the
gospel truth, each recurrence of the blood libel charge added to
its credence, thus prompting yet more accusations. This vicious
cycle continued to spiral.

There were a few emperors and enlightened Christian clergy
such as Emperor Frederick II and Pope Innocent IV who
declared that the blood libel was baseless and false. Yet neither
these rare proclamations nor the vehement denial of respected
rabbis could mitigate the monstrosity of the charge or the
frequency of its occurrence. From the twelfth century on, not a
single generation of European Jewry was spared. During the
Middle Ages, in Colmar, Krems, Munich, Magdeburg and
Weissenburg, in Paris, Bern, Wurzburg and Prague, indeed in
all of Europe, the blood libel served as the pretext for the
massacre of thousands of Jews.

In 1475, a particularly notorious incident took place in Trent, Italy. On the Thursday before Easter, a Jew by the name of Samuel found the body of a Christian toddler named Simon on the banks of the river. In order to avert even the semblance of misconduct, he took the child straight to the Catholic bishop. Not surprisingly, the Jews were nevertheless accused, and many were arrested. After fifteen days of torturous interrogation, all confessed to the crime and were burned forthwith. Meanwhile, rumors began to circulate of miraculous cures attributed to the bones of little Simon, whose embalmed body had been put on display. Pilgrims flocked to this newfound "holy" shrine, and by the sixteenth century, Saint Simon was canonized as a holy martyr by Pope Gregory XIII. For centuries, Catholics the world over continued to pray to Simon as a holy saint. Only in 1965 did the Church cancel the beatification of Simon and all celebrations in his honor.

The increased persecution of the Jews was almost always accompanied by the ubiquitous blood libel accusation. As part of his plan to convince King Ferdinand and Queen Isabella to expel the Jews from Spain in 1492, Grand Inquisitor Tomas de Torquemada engineered a blood libel case in the town of La Guardia, in which converted Jews were forced to confess under torture that the chief rabbi of the Jews had helped them abuse and crucify an innocent Christian victim. Wherever the Jew fled, the blood libel accusation followed, with all of its political, economic and social ramifications. The Jew was the perennial pariah, the perfect scapegoat, putty in the hands of those who wanted to foment anti-Semitic sentiments. Whether it was at the hands of the Poles or the Cossacks, the Ukrainians or the Tartars, the Jews were mercilessly slaughtered time and time again.

In a famous case in Damascus, Syria, in 1840, a Christian monk disappeared. The French consul confided to the Syrian authorities that a Jew was probably responsible for the crime and that the innocent monk had probably been murdered as part of a religious ceremony. Many Jews were arrested and tortured, and more than sixty Jewish children were held hostage to coerce the confession of their parents. Prominent Jews around the world, including Sir Moses Montefiore, lodged horrified protests, and ultimately, except for two who died and others who were permanently disabled, the Jews were spared. Nevertheless, the incident introduced the blood libel to the Arab world, where it has maintained credence ever since.

The blood libel has stubbornly persisted into modern times, gaining new impetus from the anti-Semitic propaganda of Nazi Germany. It has even reared its ugly head in the United States. But it is in Russia that this medieval canard found its most comfortable home during the last two centuries.

Russian Anti-Semitism

Although some Jewish communities probably graced the northern shores of the Black Sea almost twenty centuries ago, their numbers were undoubtedly very small. As persecutions of the Jews throughout Western Europe increased, however, a limited Jewish flight deep into this region began, especially from the seventh to the tenth century. Russia did not accord these Jews a very warm welcome. The Jews were thus seen as harbingers of ill. Most times, they were excluded altogether. At other times, they suffered greatly. In the sixteenth century, Czar Ivan IV, known to history as "Ivan the Terrible," ordered the drowning of all Jews who lived in territory annexed to his kingdom unless they converted to Christianity. In 1648 and 1649, the infamous years of *Tach* and *Tat*, genocidal massacres perpetrated during Bogdan Chmielnicki's Cossack uprising devastated the Jewish communities of the Ukraine.

Even in times when the Jews proved themselves an economic asset, it was often decided that it was better not to profit from a sinful enemy of the church. By 1742, all Jews who remained in the realm were expelled, and towards the end of the eighteenth century, less than 100,000 Jews lived in all of Russia.

The situation in neighboring Poland, however, was different. In the thirteenth century, in an effort to improve the economic condition of his impoverished land, King Boleslav the Pious invited Jews from across Europe to come and settle in Poland. Except for sporadic flare-ups, the masses of Jews from the hostile West who sought haven in Poland enjoyed relative freedom and prosperity for almost four hundred years until the decline of the Polish kingdom in the seventeenth century. In 1792, the dismemberment of Poland by Austria, Prussia and Russia began. By the third and final partition of Poland in 1795, after which Poland ceased to exist as a sovereign nation until 1918, over one million unwanted and despised Jews found themselves living under the iron fist of the Russian Czar.

One of the first Russian responses to its Jewish problem was the designation of a large ghetto-like district. All Jews were ordered to move to this district, known as the Pale of Settlement, which reached from the Black Sea to the Baltic and included the districts that had formed the western boundary of Russia and the eastern provinces of Poland. Even within the Pale, the Jews were restricted as to where they could live, where they could travel and how they could earn a livelihood. Decrees such as the first "Jewish Statute" of 1804, for example, prohibited settlement in villages. Before long, the Jews of the Pale found themselves constrained and subjugated in almost every aspect of their lives.

By the nineteenth century, the new spirit of enlightenment and the ideals of freedom and equality dramatically altered the existing political and social order. The American and French Revolutions had brought an end to the totalitarian rule of once-powerful monarchs, and the eastward advance of Napoleon carried the light of modern civilization into the black abyss of backward Russian medievalism and its autocratic regime. Fearing that the oppressed peoples of Russia, and especially the despised Jews, might be tempted by these revolutionary rumblings, Czar Alexander I issued even more restrictive absolutist decrees designed to crush any opposition and safeguard his throne. After his death, his successor, Czar Nicholas I, proved to be cut of the same cloth, and the Jews were offered no reprieve.

In 1827, Czar Nicholas I instituted Russia's notorious "Cantonist" conscription decree. All eligible Russian young men were required to join the military service of the Czar at the age of eighteen for a period of twenty-five years, but a quota of young Jewish boys were to be drafted at the age of twelve, to spend an additional six years in "training" in small military camps, or "cantons."

For a high percentage of these precious, painfully young Jewish children, this was an immediate death sentence, as many perished on the march to the camp itself, unable to endure the harsh conditions. For those who survived, conversion to Christianity was a foregone conclusion, for few were able to withstand, either physically or spiritually, the torments to which they were subjected. Especially onerous was the twist that it was the responsibility of the established Jewish leadership to insure that the quota was fulfilled. Even though it is estimated that at most there were "only" 60,000 actual victims over a thirty-year period, the damage was massive. Families were devastated and communities were destroyed as leaders agonized over who should live or die; fathers stopped at nothing in an attempt to spare their own sons, even at the expense of others. This evil decree of the Czar, perhaps more than any other, broke the back of Jewish resolve, undermined the legitimacy of the established leadership and destroyed community cohesiveness.

It was also during the reign of Nicholas I that the blood libel achieved new fame.

In 1799, four Jews were arrested near Vitebsk on the evening before Passover and charged with ritually murdering a Christian woman. They were ultimately released for lack of evidence, yet an official opinion was submitted to the Czar informing him that there existed a people in his realm who did, indeed, perpetrate such crimes. It was a topic that was researched and debated at the highest levels of government.

Through 1816, there were several instances of blood libel prosecutions resulting in much terror and suffering, yet mercifully, all charges were found to be baseless. In 1817, Czar Alexander I issued a circular outlawing the blood libel indictment, only to rescind it when Jewish leaders were blamed for the death of a Christian child in Velizh. With the approval of Czar Nicholas I, more blood libel charges were prosecuted in Telz in 1827 and in the district of Volhynia in 1830. A secret government commission issued a document in 1844 that detailed how and why Christian blood was used by the Jews. In 1853, two Jews of Saratov were actually convicted of ritually slaughtering two Christian children.

The blood libel had always been an integral ingredient in the castigation of the Jew, but under Nicholas I, it assumed a semi-official status. In the past, village monks had been primarily responsible for the dissemination of these vicious accusations. However, once government endorsement of anti-Semitic activities became known, many different segments of Russian society took advantage of the malice these lies generated to provoke a variety of public outrages against the Jews. A new wave of blood libels in Poland and elsewhere in Europe further inflamed the already volatile situation in Russia.

As a result of the hostility against Jews fomented by the persistent blood libels, Nicholas I was able to continue his assimilationist agenda with ease. In 1844, he issued a decree that established official government schools whose sole purpose was to estrange Jewish children from their religion. As an added burden, these schools were to be financed by a "candle" tax that was imposed upon the already indigent religious community. In an effort to further pauperize what was left of the shattered Jewish economy, all Jews were divided into two classes, "useful" and "non-useful," the latter being a sentence tantamount to extreme impoverishment, starvation or death. With the advent of the Crimean War, the Czar tripled the quota for conscription and gave the army permission to seize any Jewish child or traveler that lacked sufficient documentation.

When Nicholas I finally died in 1855, his successor, Czar Alexander II, who is portrayed as the great reformer in Russian history for his emancipation of the serfs in 1861, believed that the key to a successful assimilation of the Jews was through the adoption of a "milder" policy. The "Cantonist" laws were replaced with a general draft, whereby thousands of Jews were forced to serve in the army of the Czar, but "only" for a period of four years. Certain groups of "useful" Jews were even allowed admittance into the universities as part of an overall program to separate the Jew from his traditional moorings. Many Jews, feeling that Jewish emancipation would soon follow, leaped at the opportunity and soon distinguished themselves in many areas of Russian society. They had failed to anticipate, however, that this newfound prominence would cause a sharp and immediate reaction from the Russian people, who still did not want the Jew to live, much less prosper, in their midst.

Notwithstanding the emigration of hundreds of thousands of Jews to America (from 1880 to 1920 there would be three million), the Jewish population of the Pale had exploded to over five million by the late 1800s. As far as the gentile was concerned, these numbers meant that the Jewish problem posed a greater menace than ever, and many segments of the Russian people sought to rid themselves of the Jews. They would soon be given the opportunity.

Although there had been reforms, Alexander II was still a despot who held tight rein over a backward, feudal society and a corrupt aristocracy whose abuse of its millions of impoverished peasants was legendary. In March, 1881, the Czar was assassinated by revolutionaries. The country was in a turmoil, and a scapegoat was needed. The new successor, Czar Alexander III, was quick to spread the idea that the Jews and not the Czars were responsible for the suffering of the Russian people; the Jews were the revolutionaries bent upon the destruction of Mother Russia.

This was not a novel approach. Tremendous forces of change were sweeping through Europe as industrialization, imperialism, the power of money and the power of the machine wreaked havoc with the existing social structure. The feudal, agrarian medieval empires were dying, to the utter dismay of its aristocratic and ecclesiastical masters, and the Jew presented the perfect prey upon whom all sides could vent their frustrations. This scenario had already occurred in Germany under Bismarck and would soon repeat itself in the Dreyfus Affair in France. The Czar responded in Russia by continuing to incite pogroms and increasing the severity of his restrictions against the Jews, who were then held responsible for these outrages that "they brought upon themselves."

An adamant advocate of the divine right of kings and a fanatic adherent to the tenets of the Russian Orthodox Church, Czar Alexander III eschewed the reforms of his predecessor and instead passionately pursued his goal of restoring absolute control to the monarchy. To accomplish this, he strove to eliminate those who disagreed with his vision and to rid his kingdom of all alien influences. The Jews fell into both categories. Anti-Semitic propaganda proliferated as the government vigorously strove to cause "one-third of the Jews to assimilate, one-third to emigrate and one-third to perish." In few periods of history have the Jews been more persecuted or more maligned than they were during this period, which is why no one could have imagined that when Alexander III died in 1894, his oldest son, Czar Nicholas II would be worse.

The great masses of the Russian people were peasants and laborers who had suffered for centuries in abject poverty and ignorance. A terrible famine in 1891 further exacerbated their misery. The ruthless tyranny of the Czars ultimately led to the growth of anarchists, terrorists, communists, socialists and all manner of other radicals, who spurred a widespread opposition movement. These group attracted many Jewish revolutionaries to whom a drastic change also seemed to provide the only solution to their unmitigated persecution. They dreamed of a glorious new era of equal rights and social justice that could only come with the downfall of the Czar.

In desperation, the new Czar also turned to the age-old strategy of attempting to redirect popular discontent onto a convenient scapegoat. The Jew, the "murderous, blood-sucking, money-hungry fiend," was now a "subversive revolutionary" as well. The Jew was once again the culprit that all sides could blame. "Drown the revolution in Jewish blood!" became the battle cry that ultimately erupted during Passover of 1903 in the Kishinev pogrom, notorious for its violence and bloodshed.

Russia seethed with unrest. There were more assassinations and bombings—and more pogroms. Russian society was being shaken to its very foundations. The entry into the Russo-Japanese War of 1903-05, which was intended to help restore the Czar's prestige and unite the country, resulted in a disastrous loss. Violent strikes and terrible uprisings followed until January of

1905, when, in front of the winter palace, government troops opened fire upon workers who had come to petition the Czar for a constitution. Over a thousand were massacred on that "Bloody Sunday."

In October of 1905, the workers finally revolted and organized a nationwide strike. To avert an all-out civil war between the privileged and the protesters, the frightened Czar temporarily yielded to the demands of the liberals. He signed the October Manifesto, creating an elected parliament called the Duma, and he granted the country a limited constitution.

While ending the immediate violence, these democratic concessions failed to bridge the deep chasms that had formed within Russian society. For the radicals, these reforms were not nearly enough; they intended to use whatever newfound freedom they had acquired to continue their struggle. On the other hand, those who supported the Czar—the Church, the nobility and the landed proprietors—were determined to maintain their stranglehold on the people and resist reform at all cost; any attempt to address the genuine grievances of the people was met with opposition and oppression. A key component of this reaction to the revolution was the plan to convince the peasants that the revolutionary movement was a Jewish movement destined to destroy all of Russia. If the revolution could thus be discredited, the Czar reasoned, the masses of the Russians would turn to him for protection against this common foe.

To further arouse the passions of the people against the Jew, the government became involved in the production of incendiary literature. From 1905-1916, detailed records reveal that 14,327,000 copies of 2,837 anti-Semitic pamphlets were written and distributed by various government officials, and many of them were printed in the offices of the Ministry of the Interior. The Czar himself contributed over twelve million rubles from his private purse for the publication of one particularly noxious work, *The Protocols of the Elders of Zion*, a forgery concocted by the Russian secret police from old German and French lies. This tract purportedly contained secret notes detailing the inner workings of an international Jewish conspiracy to take over the world. The Czar was so genuinely convinced of the existence of a universal Jewish alliance, which possessed tremendous financial resources, that he conducted private negotiations with the Kaiser of Germany and the Vatican on how to deal with this imminent threat.

The plan for the government's counteroffensive to the revolution was in place. The Minister of the Interior was in charge of organizing pogroms, and the Minister of Justice was responsible for pardoning all who might be found guilty of robbing or killing a Jew. To help the Czar carry out the "holy" work of purging the motherland of her enemies, there arose a paramilitary organization called the Black Hundreds, which was composed of hoodlums organized into cadres one hundred strong to carry out the dictates of the Czar. All was ready.

In 1905, during the last week of October and the first week of November, six hundred and sixty Jewish communities were attacked. In Odessa alone, three hundred victims were killed, thousands maimed and over forty thousand financially wiped out. The modern world recoiled in horror as the Czar honored the leaders of the Black Hundreds, rewarding them for their loyal service to the Russian people. By the time brutal pogroms took place in Bialystok and Siedlce in 1906, the Czar was able to involve his army openly and actively.

From the beginning, the Duma posed a problem for the Czar. The first Duma, to which twelve Jews had been elected, appointed a committee to investigate the pogrom that had occurred in Bialystok in 1906. Several liberal members of the parliament, including the twelve Jews, signed a report that held government officials responsible for the carnage. The Czar branded the signatories traitors and threw them all into prison. He also promptly dissolved the Duma and called for new elections.

Of the four Jews elected to the second Duma, two were soon assassinated by the Black Hundreds. The Czar dissolved the second Duma in 1907, and the third Duma was nothing more that a forum for militant, nationalistic ranting against all who were not true Russians and loyal to their Czar. The Jewish people were, of course, singled out. In February of 1911, in a speech entered into the official record of the third Duma, a representative stated, "The Jewish race is a criminal race that hates mankind . . . they must remain subjugated by all the restrictions established in the past . . . The Jewish force is extraordinary, and the State alone is powerful enough to resist this dreadful power."

For decades, the government had defended its persecutions of Jews by emphasizing their role in the revolutionary movement. The official government position was that anti-Jewish pogroms were merely spontaneous "outbursts of popular indignation" against the Jewish rebels. However, since increasing numbers of Russians were joining the ranks of the opposition, this official explanation was no longer adequate. The Russian people needed a stronger motivation to ally themselves with the Czar, even if it was in his struggle with the Jew. The Czar needed to persuade his Russian subjects that no civilized society could tolerate such a race in its midst. The Czar would further have to convince them that only he could save them from the danger the Jew posed. He hoped a renewal of the heinous blood libel accusation, on a scale never before attempted, could accomplish this feat. The wheels were set in motion.

A report issued by the Congress of the Nobility soon thereafter took the position that the war against the Jews must be continued until they were all annihilated, since their religion "teaches its adherents to be bloodthirsty, cruel and criminal, even to the point of murdering Christian children." The press release of a right wing organization more graphically stated that "the government must recognize that the Jews are dangerous to the life of mankind in the same measure as wolves, scorpions, reptiles, poisonous spiders and similar creatures, which are destroyed because they are deadly for human beings . . . Jews must be placed under such conditions that they will die out. This is the present task of the government and of the best men in the country."

On March 19, 1911, the newspaper *Zemshtchina* warned the public that it would be impossible to restore any rights to the Jews, for they were too dangerous. Not coincidentally, on March 20, the head of the Nationalist faction in the Duma stated that he considered it his mission to see that all Jews were again confined to the Pale and totally "eliminated from the schools, the courts and the press." The noose was tightening rapidly.

On that very same day, March 20, 1911, it was reported that

the dead body of a boy by the name of Andrei Yustchinsky had been found on the outskirts of Kiev. The stage was thus set for what was to be one of the most infamous blood libel accusations in history.

Shari Schwartz
Marcheshvan, 5753 (1992)
Brooklyn, New York

SCAPEGOAT ON TRIAL

The story of

MENDEL BEILIS

CHAPTER 1

War and Peace

In 1894, when Czar Nicholas II ascended the Russian throne, the Jews were most hopeful that it would bode well for them. It was rumored that Nicholas had been chastised by his own father Czar Alexander III on account of his friendliness towards the Jews. Some even said that he had intended to marry a Jewish girl. As a result of these stories, at the very least, the Jews had visions of a sympathetic ruler who might relieve them of their suffering. Surely, he would be just and merciful.

History has revealed how unfounded these hopes turned out to be. The real suffering that the Jews experienced during his reign is well known to the world.* Tragically, it was my misfortune, more than anyone else's, to feel the weight of his

---

* Czar Nicholas II turned out to be a much-hated, brutal anti-Semite. The last Romanov emperor, he was executed during the Russian Revolution.

royal wrath. Why I in particular should have been selected for this role is one of the secrets of Providence.

About a year after I had returned from my period of military service,* I married and settled in Mezhigorye, a town about eight miles from Kiev. I found a position at a brick-kiln which belonged to my wife's uncle. I lived a peaceful and uneventful life.

Some time later, I received a letter from a cousin of mine. He offered me the superintendentship of a brick-kiln that was about to be built. My cousin was the superintendent of a hospital for the poor in Kiev, and the patron benefactor of this hospital was a man by the name of Zaitzev, the famous magnate in the sugar industry. In order to establish a perpetual endowment for the hospital, Mr. Zaitzev decided to build a brick-kiln, the profits of which would go towards the maintenance of the hospital. Since my cousin was totally unfamiliar with the brick manufacturing business, he thought of me. I felt that such a position in Kiev would offer me better opportunity. Therefore, I accepted the position.

The factory, of which I became the overseer, was situated on the borderline between two city districts. One district was named Plossky and the other Lukianovsky. The Jews only had the right to reside in the Plossky district. Zaitzev's hospital and my cousin's residence were both located within the boundary of this

---

* Even though the dreaded Cantonist Laws, which had required conscription of a quota of Jewish boys, some only twelve years old, into the service of the Czar for periods of twenty-five years, were no longer in effect, the military draft was still a terrible ordeal that resulted in the death and coerced conversion of many young Jewish men.

district. However, the factory itself was located outside the Pale,* which meant that Jews were forbidden to live there. It was only due to Zaitzev's influence that I, as a Jew, was permitted to live on such sacred ground. Since he was a merchant of what was known as the First Guild, Russian law permitted him to have a Jewish employee. Out of a population of ten thousand people that lived in the vicinity of the factory, I was the only Jew. In spite of this, I did not have any problems, even though about five hundred non-Jews worked in the factory.

My personal contact with the Russians in the area was very limited. My work was restricted to the office, where I was in charge of the selling and the shipping. I never experienced any difficulty with the Russians who lived in the neighborhood. There was only one exception, which occurred during the Revolution, in 1905.** When a torrent of pogroms*** swept through every Jewish town, I also was in danger. However, the local Russian priest came to my rescue. He demanded that since I was the only Jew in the district, I should receive a special guard.

He showed me this kindness as a reward for a favor I had once done for him. The priest was the director of a local orphanage, and when it was being built, he had come to me and requested that I sell him bricks at a cheaper rate. I earned his

---

* Beginning in 1795, it was decreed by the Czar that the entire Jewish population within his domain must be confined to an area called the "Pale of Settlement."
** After the humiliating defeat of the Czar in the Russo-Japanese War of 1904, terrible civil strife ensued. Much of the blame fell on the Jews.
*** Officially incited "spontaneous" mob rampages that sanctioned murder and destruction of defenseless Jewish inhabitants.

gratitude by taking the matter up with Mr. Zaitzev, who finally agreed to sell him the bricks at a very low price.

There was also another reason for the priest's indebtedness to me. Some distance from our factory there was another one owned by a Russian named Shevtchenko. The most direct route to the district cemetery passed through the grounds of both these factories. When I first came to the town, the priest had asked me for permission to allow the various funeral processions to pass through the factory grounds. I consented to his request. When Shevtchenko was asked for permission to pass through his property, he refused. The priest often spoke of this incident to his fellow Russians, saying, "You see, the Christian did not give me permission, yet the Jew did."

And thus I lived at the factory for about fifteen years, enjoying the advantages of living near a large city. For example, one of my boys was able to attend a government gymnasium.* The younger ones attended the *cheder*, the religious school. It is true that it was quite a distance from the factory to the city, but what more could one ask? I thanked the Lord for what I had and was content with my life. After all, I had a secure, respectable position. Everything seemed to indicate that my future would be filled with peace and happiness. I expected to spend the rest of my days in contentment. Who could have known that the demon of destruction was dancing behind me, jeering at all my hopes and plans?

In 1911, I was plunged into a swirl of misfortune. Such misfortune I shall never forget, for it destroyed my life forever.

---

* The European term for the more prestigious college-preparatory secondary school.

CHAPTER 2

A Boy Is Murdered

Though fourteen years have passed since those dreadful days, the old scenes stand out with remarkable vividness, as if they had been etched on my brain. It was the 20th of March, and everything seemed perfectly normal. The dawn had not yet broken when I got up and went to the office. The window which I used to face while at my desk overlooked the street.

As I looked through the window on that cold, dark morning, I saw people hurrying somewhere, all in one direction. It was not unusual to see individual workers coming to the factory at that time of the morning, and sometimes there was even an occasional passerby. But on that particular day the people appeared in large groups, walking rapidly, coming from various streets. I went outside to discover the cause of the commotion, and I was told by one of the crowd that the body of a murdered child had been found in the vicinity.

Within a few hours, the papers carried the news that the body of a Russian boy named Andriusha Yustchinsky had been found within a half mile of the factory. The mutilated body of the murdered boy was discovered in a cave, where it had apparently been deposited.

That evening, one of my Russian neighbors, a member of the Black Hundreds,* came to visit me. He declared that according to the newspaper published by his organization this was not the usual kind of murder, that the Yustchinsky child had been murdered by Jews for purposes of a religious ritual.** The newspaper, which went by the name of the organization, was patriotically dedicated to saving Russia from the Jews.

The ordinary Russians, however, unconcerned with such fanatical plans for the salvation of Russia, were saying that the murder had been committed by Yustchinsky's mother and a certain woman whose name was Vera Tchebiriak. Suspicion at once centered on Yustchinsky's mother because she had not displayed any anxiety about her son's disappearance. The Yustchinsky boy had disappeared on the 12th of March and was found on the 20th. How could she, his mother, explain her failure to notify the police at once of his disappearance? She had also failed to show any interest in finding him. Furthermore, she hadn't displayed any signs of grief when her son's murdered

* Notoriously violent, anti-Semitic, paramilitary groups of 100 thugs who were organized in the aftermath of the 1905 Revolution to harass and persecute anyone not unswervingly loyal to the Czar.
** The body had been found on March 20, 1911. By March 21, anonymous letters signed "a Christian" were sent across Russia to the police, state attorneys, the press, relatives of the boy, everywhere, exclaiming that the murder was the work of the Jews.

body was discovered. The neighbors were quick to comment on these peculiarities, and as time went on, their suspicions increased.

There was another reason why the boy's mother was suspected of having been involved with the murder. Andriusha Yustchinsky's father had been killed in the Russo-Japanese War* and had left his son five hundred rubles, which the bank had been holding in trust for the boy until he would come of age. In the meantime, Andriusha's mother had found a mate for herself, and this fellow was rather upset that he could not get his hands on those five hundred rubles. These were just some of the reasons that caused people to suspect that Yustchinsky's mother was involved in the murder.

This Vera Tchebiriak, who was notorious around Lukianovsky, was also the focus of much suspicion. Her husband was a clerk at the telegraph office and was seldom home, even at night. She was known to have dealings with a gang of thieves who were not ordinary lawbreakers. They used to dress royally, sometimes even appearing in officers' uniforms. Her brother Singayevsky and two other friends, named Latischeff and Rudzinsky, were members of this gang. They would do the stealing, and she would sell the loot. The neighbors were fully aware of her nefarious activities, but no one dared interfere.

It was known that Vera's own son Zhenia was Andriusha's schoolmate and that they were both thirteen years old. They would often spend the night together at the Tchebiriak house. If

---

* In an attempt to both halt Japanese expansion and quell revolutionary aspirations by uniting the country against a common foe, the Czar, ill-advised and unprepared, led a mutinous military into a disastrous war.

on one of these overnight visits Andriusha had witnessed some criminal act, then the thieves might have felt the need to silence him. The police had another reason for suspecting Tchebiriak of complicity. Hundreds of people had come to see Yustchinsky's body, and because of his swollen face, not one of them had been able to recognize him. However, Vera Tchebiriak recognized him at once, and this immediately aroused further suspicion.

Tchebiriak lived in a house that belonged to a Russian by the name of Zakhartchenko, who lived close to our factory and was himself a member of the Black Hundreds. Zakhartchenko often used to confide in me how happy he would be to get rid of Tchebiriak. He was, however, afraid to start trouble. He told me several times after the murder that he felt certain it had taken place in Tchebiriak's house, a veritable den of crime.

Vera Tchebiriak was finally arrested. A few days later, the Moscow police arrested three suspicious young men. Since they were found to be residents of Kiev, they were sent to that city. Upon examination, it was found that they had left Kiev on March 12, the day of Yustchinsky's disappearance and that, on the same day, they had spent some time in Vera's house. As a matter of fact, these men were actually the leaders of her gang.

When the policemen of Lukianovsky were brought to Kiev to identify the apprehended trio, the police were terribly frightened. They realized that these arrested men were the same men that they had often seen parading in officers' uniforms. They had believed that these men were genuine officers and had even extended to them the officers' salute. The police had known that these "gentlemen" used to visit Tchebiriak's house, but they had never doubted their authenticity.

By the time the funeral took place, which was just one week after the body was found, handbills calling upon Christians to exterminate the Jews were already being circulated.* The Jews were accused of having slain Yustchinsky, because his blood was needed for the Jewish Passover.** The pamphlets proclaimed that his blood must be avenged. This was the first attempt to direct attention away from the real culprits and to start the religious pot boiling in order to divert well-founded suspicions.

When these three gang leaders were arrested, a powerful group within the Black Hundreds organization named the Double-Headed Eagle continued their incendiary activities and issued a loud cry of indignation.

"What a public scandal!" they proclaimed. "Is it possible that the Jews who have murdered Yustchinsky should be allowed to go scot-free, while such innocent persons are imprisoned? Let the child be taken out of his grave, and let the world see how the body was stabbed by the Jews."

The uproar caused by the Black Hundreds had its effect. The boy's body was disinterred, and after examination, the notorious Professor Sikorsky declared that it was no usual murder. He

---

* Professionally printed pamphlets claiming that Jews are a "criminal species that brings death to any wholesome society" were circulated in Kiev and St. Petersburg. Newspaper columns similarly described in gruesome detail how the Jews had murdered this child. The articles concluded that the Jews must be deprived of all rights and dealt with once and for all.

** Passover is the Jewish festival commemorating the exodus from Egypt. As a part of the observance, matzah, a cracker-like unleavened bread, is eaten. For generations Jews had been tortured and killed for allegedly murdering Christian children in order to use their blood to bake this Passover matzah. This was the infamous blood libel.

concluded that the murder had been committed for religious purposes. He based this on the discovery of thirteen stab wounds, which, he said, was a religiously significant number.

In the beginning, it all seemed so ludicrous. Everyone had been certain that the crime was the work of Tchebiriak's gang. There was more than enough proof to support that contention. Then people came along with fantastic tales of thirteen stab wounds and mysterious religious rituals.

Unfortunately, it soon proved to be no joke. The Black Hundreds had devised a devilish plot against the Jews, and since these pogromists exercised a powerful influence at the time, they energetically proceeded to implement their scheme.

CHAPTER 3

Arrested at Dawn

The case was taken over by Investigating Attorney Fenenko. He began to visit our neighborhood frequently. He measured the distances from the cave where Yustchinsky's body had been found to both the factory and to Tchebiriak's house. In this manner, he investigated the murder for several months.

As the pogromists' newspapers continued whitewashing the gang of thieves and throwing accusations at the Jewish people, Russian detectives began to visit our factory. They asked my children if they had known the Yustchinsky boy and if they used to play with him. One of the detectives took up residence in the house opposite ours and watched wherever I went and whatever I did. I was informed that the detectives, seeing that their investigation had not been productive, began to treat the Russian children to sweets to make them say that Andriusha used to visit us and that my children had played with him.

After a while, a detective named Polishtchuk began to visit me rather frequently. He once told me that there was a feeling that the crime had been committed on the factory premises and that, furthermore, I must have been involved. On the morning following my conversation with Polishtchuk, a squad of about ten persons appeared at the factory, accompanied by Fenenko, the Investigating Attorney. Fenenko appeared in the best of moods when he began to question me.

"You are the manager of this factory?"

"Yes."

"Since when?"

"For about fifteen years."

"Are there any other Jews here besides you?"

"No. I am here alone."

"You are a Jew, are you not? Where do you go to pray? Is there a synagogue here?"

"I am a Jew, but there is no synagogue here. One can pray at home as well."

"Do you observe the Sabbath?"

"The factory is kept running on Saturdays, so I do not leave the grounds."

"Have you a cow?" he suddenly asked. "Do you sell any milk?"

"I have a cow," I replied. "But I do not sell milk. We need all of it for our family."

"And let us say, a good friend of yours comes to you, do you sell him a glass of milk?"

"When a good friend of mine comes to me, I give him food and drink, including milk, but I never sell it."

I simply could not understand the necessity of these questions about my piety and as to whether I went to a synagogue. Had the authorities become so pious that they could not tolerate my praying without an official *minyan*, a group of ten men required by Jewish law? And what was the purpose of all these questions about the cow and the milk?

Fenenko and his confreres seemed quite satisfied and bid me a cordial good-bye. As they were leaving, I noticed that one of them photographed me. Evidently, they were quite meticulous about their work. This incident occurred on Thursday, July 21, 1911, on the 9th of *Av*, a day of fasting for the Jews, when we bewail our great misfortunes, the destruction of the Temple and our exile from our homeland, from Zion. This date marks the anniversary of our sufferings in exile.

At dawn, on Friday, July 22, when everyone was still fast asleep, I heard a great commotion involving many horses and men. Before I had a chance to look out, there was a loud banging on the door. Naturally, I was quite alarmed. What could have happened at this time of the morning? In all the fifteen years I had lived at the factory, I had never heard such noise. In the meantime, the knocking grew louder.

My first thought was that a fire had broken out at the factory. I rushed to the window, and although it was quite dark, I could recognize the familiar uniforms of the gendarmes. What could gendarmes be doing here at night? Why all that knocking at the door? Everything turned dark before my eyes. My head swam. I nearly swooned with fright. The incessant knocking, however, made me realize that this was no time for reflection, and I rushed to open the door.

A large squad of gendarmes burst in, led by Colonel Kuliabko, the notorious chief of the Okhrana, the secret political police. After placing a guard at the door, Colonel Kuliabko walked right up to me.

"Are you Beilis?" he snarled.

"Yes."

"In the name of His Majesty, you are arrested," thundered his diabolical voice. "Get dressed."

In the meantime, my wife and children awoke and began to wail. The children were frightened by the uniforms and the swords, and they were tugging with all their might for me to protect them. The poor children did not understand that their father was helpless and himself in need of protection.

I was forcibly jerked away from my family and no one was allowed to come near me. I was not even permitted to utter a word to my wife. In silence, restraining my tears, I dressed myself, and without being allowed to reassure my children or kiss them goodbye, I was taken away by the police.

I was taken to the headquarters of the Okhrana, but the colonel remained behind to search my home. As I was taken into the street outside, I met many of the workers going toward the factory. I felt ashamed and asked the police to let me walk on the sidewalk instead of in the street, which was the custom when police escorted arrested persons. They refused.

I later learned that ironically, precisely at the time of my incarceration, Vera Tchebiriak and her gang of thieves, along with Madame Yushtchinsky, were released from prison as wrongly suspected, innocent persons. I wondered what would become of me.

CHAPTER 4

The Secret Police

It was still quiet in the Okhrana when we arrived. As a rule, the Russian officials did not care to get up too early. The desk sergeant was busy with his books and issuing orders to some clerks and spies, who looked at me with cunning and piercing eyes.

My life was spent in such an ordinary way, that I never imagined I would be arrested* and have to sit in the Okhrana, watched by a *gorodovoy*, who would not take his eyes from me even for a single second. But as the saying goes, there is no

---

* Although it may be difficult for the reader to understand how Beilis could have been so naive after all that had transpired, it must be remembered that he has recounted these events with the benefit of hindsight. At the time, he was truly overwhelmed by the circumstances, and it was impossible for him to have imagined that in the twentieth century he could have been implicated for such a murder.

foolproof insurance against prison and death.

I sat there in a feverish state, hot and cold at the same time, with a fierce headache. I heard the stamping of horses' hooves followed by the tinkling of spurs in the hall. The door opened, and the gendarmes, who had remained in my house for the search, entered. Seeing that the gendarmes were alone, I felt more assured. Then tea was brought in, and I was asked whether I would like something to eat. I declined, thanking them for their courtesy. Even though my tongue was dry as hot sand, I could not touch the tea. All that time I kept thinking, "What is going to happen next? Why have I been arrested?"

Finally, Colonel Kuliabko came in. He handed me a large sheet of paper that was a questionnaire. I was told to answer the following questions: Who are you? From where do you come? Who is your father? What is your religion? Do you have any relatives?

And finally, there was the question: What do you know about Yustchinsky's murder?

Before he left the room, Kuliabko told me, "When you have answered the questions, ring the bell, and I'll come back."

When I read the last question, I felt as if there was a knife at my throat. At last I understood what had happened. I tried to find consolation in the form of the question: "What did I know about the murder?" Maybe, I would be no more than a witness.

I answered all the questions. As for the murder, I stated that I knew nothing beyond what people in the street were saying about it. Who had perpetrated it? And for what purpose? I did not know.

I rang the bell. Kuliabko entered and looked over my replies.

"Is this all?" he shouted. "Nonsense. If you don't tell me the truth, I'll send you up to the Petropavlovsky fortress." (This was a well known and much feared political prison in Petrograd.) He banged the door furiously and left the room.

About four o'clock in the afternoon, I heard the weeping of a child that sounded like my own. I finally recognized the voice of one of my children. Out of sheer desperation, I began to knock my head against the wall. I knew that my son was very timid and nervous and that he was especially afraid of the police. I actually feared that he might die in their hands.

While he was crying, the door opened, and Kuliabko re-entered the room.

"See, your boy is also telling lies," he said.

"What lies?" I entreated.

"Zhenia, come in!" He brought Tchebiriak's son into the room, and turning towards me, he snapped, "Zhenia says that your boy used to play with Andriusha, and your boy denies it."

Thereupon, the colonel led the Tchebiriak boy out of the room. A few minutes later, I heard footsteps in the hall. I looked through the grating and saw the *gorodovoy* leading my eight-year-old son away. I felt a violent tug at my heart as I saw the *gorodovoy* lock him in one of the cells. Initially, I had expected to be held for a few hours, interrogated and finally released. I was innocent, and they were bound to see that a mistake had occurred. But now, I didn't know what to expect. I was only preoccupied with thoughts of my child. Why had they brought him into this hell?

That evening, a Russian woman came in and said to me, "Your child is here, but have no fear. I am looking after him. Please don't worry. I am a mother myself. I understand your suffering and sympathize with you. Don't worry. God saves the honest man."

As nighttime approached, I realized it was Friday night and I would not be able to celebrate the Sabbath. I thought of what my Friday nights were usually like, with the candles on the table and the children dressed in their Sabbath best. Everyone was so warm and friendly. And now? The house was in shambles, and my wife must be beside herself with fear. There was no light, no joy. I knew my loved ones were weeping their eyes out. I almost forgot my own troubles, thinking of my imprisoned son and my mourning family. I rang the bell, and Kuliabko came in.

"Listen," I said to him. "I don't care what happens to me. The truth will win out and I'll be released, but why keep my child a prisoner? You are yourself a father. My child could get sick here, and it will be on your conscience. Can't you release my son?"

He shot me a smile. "All you have to do is tell me the truth."

"What do you want, truth or falsehood?" I cried passionately. "Even if you insisted, I couldn't tell you a lie. I am innocent!"

"Nonsense, nonsense," he nonchalantly replied, dismissing the thought with a whisk of his hand. "I'll just send you to jail, and then you'll change your story."

He went out with the usual banging of the door, and I remained alone. All along, I had anticipated that at any moment, in just one more minute, I would be freed. But when I heard the clock strike midnight, I realized I was expected to spend the night in that place. I could not sleep. From time to time, I heard the coughing of my son, and it made my brain reel.

Saturday morning, the Russian woman came in again and told me she had slept in the same room with my child. About noon, I heard someone ask my son, "Will you be able to get home by yourself, or shall I send a man to take you?"

An hour later, a *gorodovoy* came into my room and told me that he had taken my son to the streetcar, but the boy had refused to board it, running home on foot instead.* Just knowing my son was free made me happier.

Sunday, I again heard children's voices. It was my children. They must have been brought to the Okhrana for questioning. I was given permission to go out into the hall to see them, yet moments later, we were again separated.

I was kept in the Okhrana building for eight long days. None of the officials came to see me, but this only increased my anxiety. I hoped for the best but expected the worst. If they don't even ask me anything, I thought, then this could continue without end. Why? Why? On the evening of August 3, a *gorodovoy* came and told me to get ready to go to the Investigating Attorney. This news cheered me up somewhat, for it meant that at last something was happening. At the very least, I'd find out how things stood. I dressed quickly, and was escorted by two *gorodovoys* to the Attorney.

During the short time I had spent in prison, I had almost forgotten what the streets looked like. I watched the people, so carefree, passing by, and I enjoyed the freedom and light as though I had never experienced them before. I was considerably weakened by the enforced seclusion and found it rather hard to walk. I asked my guard if we could use the streetcar.

---

* To have used the streetcar would have constituted a violation of the Sabbath. Incidents such as this reveal that the Beilis family was accustomed to observing Jewish laws and customs.

"You are an arrested person, and you cannot travel with other people," one of the *gorodovoys* answered abruptly.

As we proceeded, people on the street stopped to point at me. Some even recognized me, which only added to my pain.

CHAPTER 5

Strange Questions

Exhausted by all the unwarranted insults to which I had been subjected at the Okhrana and weakened by the long march through the city under the escort of the policemen, I could hardly reach the district court. Upon our arrival, I was brought into a large hall where Investigating Attorney Fenenko, District Attorney Karbovsky and his assistant Loshkareff all awaited me.

They gave each other knowing looks, as though the outcome of the meeting was a foregone conclusion. I felt despondent, especially when I remembered the questions Fenenko had mockingly asked me at my home.

Ordinarily, the police who bring an arrested person to the *Sliedovatiel*, the Investigating Attorney, are supposed to remain on guard during the interrogation. They are not permitted to let the prisoner out of their sight. Now, however, something unusual happened. My guards were told to leave the hall. This only increased my apprehension. I knew these deceitful officials were up to some trick, but I had no choice in the matter. My feelings vacillated between hope and despair. The hope was inspired by the knowledge of my innocence, and the despair was born of my acquaintance with the Russian bureaucracy. Soon Fenenko turned to me.

"Did you know Andriusha Yustchinsky?" he asked.

"No," I replied without hesitation. "I work in the office of a large factory; my daily relations are with merchants and adults, not young children, especially street children. I might have seen him at one time, but one meets quite a few people on the street. I am certain I could not have distinguished him from any other boy."

District Attorney Karbovsky had been leaning back on his chair, watching me intently. Suddenly hunching forward over the table, he began interrogating me.

"They say there are people among you Jews who are called *tzaddikim*, pious men, and that when one wishes to do harm to another man, one goes to the *tzaddik* and gives him a *pidion*, a fee. Then the *tzaddik* uses the powers of his word to bring misfortune upon the other man."

Whenever he used Hebrew words like *tzaddik* and *pidion*, he first consulted a notebook he was holding.

"I'm sorry," I answered, "but I know nothing about *tzaddikim*, *pidionos* or any of those other things. I am a man entirely devoted to my business, and I do not understand what you want from me."

"And what are you?" he continued, as he again consulted the

notebook in his hand. "Are you a *chassid* or a *misnaged?*" *

"I am a Jew," I replied. "I don't know the difference between a *chassid* and a *misnaged.*"

"What is the thing that you Jews call an *afikoman?*" **

"I tell you, I don't know," was all I could respond.

I began to regard these men as somewhat unbalanced. What could they possibly want? What had Yustchinsky's murder to do with the *afikoman?* And furthermore, how did the difference between *chassidim* and *misnagdim* concern them? I could only imagine that they were poking fun at me and some of the Jewish rituals.

Unfortunately, they were not jesting. On the surface, they appeared to be sincere, but I thought that surely they realized that Vera Tchebiriak had murdered the boy and were only directing these questions to me on orders from some higher authority.

After the questioning, Fenenko ordered the *gorodovoys* to escort me back to the Okhrana. Although my hopes were again dashed, I believed they would soon realize their mistake and send me home.

When we reached the Okhrana, I was led into a room where I found three political prisoners, two Jews and one Russian. At that time, the Okhrana was particularly crowded because Czar Nicholas was about to come to Kiev, and it was necessary to rid

---

* The *misnaged* was the traditional orthodox European Jew, whereas the *chassid* was an adherent of a particular spiritual leader who stressed piety and worship. Noted for his distinctive garb, the *chassid* was more distrusted by the Russian authorities.

** A piece of *matzah* that is eaten at the conclusion of the Passover ceremonial meal.

the city of all the disloyal elements. When my fellow prisoners discovered who I was, they began to tell me I would soon be released and not to lose hope. Fate, however, seemed against me. I felt more despondent than ever. What could I, a helpless, friendless man, do against an organized, autocratic bureaucracy? This was not the first time the government had attempted to instigate a pogrom through some of its agents. The only thought that comforted me was knowing they did not have a vestige of proof against me.

A few days later, I was again summoned to the *Sliedovatiel*. These inquiries both intrigued and agitated me. On the one hand, I felt encouraged, for if they wanted to question me, then maybe it was a sign that they were seeking the truth. On the other hand, their bizarre questions frightened me. I suspected the questions were only designed to confuse and entangle me and were not relevant to the facts of the case. My apprehensions were further heightened when I was told by some of my fellow prisoners that the whole case smelled of politics and that the chief purpose of the whole affair was to incite pogroms against the Jews. The Minister of Justice himself, it seems, was interested in creating a Jewish case and was extending the protection of the government to the real criminals. For some strange reason, I feared Fenenko the most, although I discovered later that he had been the least hostile towards me.

When I was brought to the District Court, I found Fenenko there alone. Again, he dismissed my guard. He sat absorbed in thought for a while, then he abruptly turned towards me.

"Beilis, you must understand that it is not I who am accusing you," he said curtly. "It is the District Attorney. He is the one who has ordered your imprisonment."

"I'm going to go to prison?" I stammered in numbed disbelief. "Will I have to wear prisoner's clothes?"

"I don't know what is going to happen to you. I only want you to know that the orders are the District Attorney's and not mine."

This message was the last thing I wanted to hear. I broke out in a cold sweat and sensed that all was lost. They were putting me in prison. Terrified by the thought, I forced myself to speak up.

"May I remind you of something?" I interjected, trying to remain composed. "This is the first time in my life that I have had to deal with an official of your rank, but I know it is the duty of an Investigating Attorney to research the facts and determine the truth. When the Investigating Attorney collects all the possible evidence, he prepares an indictment and turns it over to the District Attorney. And if the evidence incriminates the suspected person, then he is imprisoned. But if there is not enough evidence, the man is set free. If you send me to prison now, that means you have found something against me. But what have I done? For what crime have I been indicted?"

"Ask me no questions," was all that Fenenko would answer. "I have told you more than enough. It is the District Attorney, not I."

I could tell from Fenenko's manner of speaking that something was going on. The whole incident seemed part of some insidious plot. I was not given much time to reflect upon the matter, for the *gorodovoy* was called in and I was taken back to the Okhrana, together with the sealed indictment.

Shortly afterwards, I was prepared for transfer to jail. At least the officials granted my request to be allowed to spend the night with the Jews whose acquaintance I had made earlier.

CHAPTER 6

Behind Bars

The guard who accompanied me back to prison allowed me to take the tramcar. However, we did not go inside and sit with the other passengers. We remained standing on the platform instead. While riding to jail, I passed some of Zaitzev's employees going to work. I even saw a few of my acquaintances. This was all I needed to make my depression complete.

During our ride, a Russian boarded the car. It was Zakhartchenko, the owner of the house where the Tchebiriaks lived. When he noticed me, he embraced me with kisses.

"Brother," he said, "don't lose spirit. I myself am a member of the Double-Headed Eagle, but I tell you that the stones of the bridge will crumble and the truth will win out." With these words he jumped off the car.

Even though he had broken the law by speaking to a prisoner, my guards let him go unharmed because he was wearing the badge of the Double Eagle. Those who bore this insignia were allowed to do whatever they pleased. The *gorodovoy* was impressed by Zakhartchenko's speech and treated me in a more friendly manner. Any humane gesture towards me by a Russian both before and during my imprisonment was greatly appreciated and somewhat mitigated the bitterness I felt for my persecutors.

We alighted from the tramcar after it stopped at the last station and continued our journey to jail on foot. When we passed by a fruit market, the *gorodovoy* went to a stall, bought some pears and offered them to me. I couldn't contain my amazement.

"I bought them for you," he said. "You are going to prison, and you can't get any there."

As soon as I entered the prison door, the official called out my name, "Beilis!" All the other officials came running out to see me. Each poked fun at me and ridiculed me with his eyes. Then one got up the courage to come closer.

"Well, here we'll feed you *matzah* and blood to your heart's content," he snarled sarcastically. "Go on, change your clothes!"

I was led into a small room where I was given my royal attire, the drab prison uniform. As I took off my boots, the blood rushed to my head. Darkness swept over me, and I felt I was going to faint. A guard came over and took off my shoes. When I was put into the chair to have my hair cut, I again felt dizzy. The same Russian guard came over and gave me some water.

Around noon, I was taken to my cell. About forty other prisoners already resided there. The door was locked behind me, and there was no way out. The room to which I had been

assigned was not one of the regular prison rooms. It belonged to
the hospital. Prisoners were required to spend thirty days in this
area before they could be transferred to the real part of the prison.
In order to survive these foul and dark quarters, one had to have
hope and remain strong, as strong as the bars of the grate. My
heart sank as I surveyed my new home and friends.

The walls were painted with tar, and hardly a ray of light
could seep through the bars. The nauseating smell of dirt and
unwashed humanity was revolting. The crowded prisoners were
jumping around, dancing and pulling crazy pranks. One was
singing a song, another was telling smutty stories and others were
wrestling and sparring. Was I condemned to live in this
atmosphere for a lifetime, or was this just part of a horrible
dream?

Fenenko's words came back to me. "It is the District
Attorney, not I."

I sat down in one of the remote corners of the room to ponder
my predicament. I was immersed in these thoughts, with my
head bent on my *chalat*, the prisoner's overcoat, when I heard
the door of the big cell open and a drunken voice call out,
"Dinner!"

When I had first entered the cell, I noticed several pails on
the floor that were like those used in bathhouses. There were
about four or five of these pails, and when the call for dinner rang
out, several prisoners rushed towards them. I was later informed
that these pails, from which we ate our food, were also used as
wash buckets for the dirty laundry from the prison.

No one fought over these pails, because there were enough
to go around. Since ten people could share one pail and since

there were about forty men in our room, the four pails we had were sufficient. The problem was that there were only three spoons. A free-for-all ensued to determine who would get to eat first. The fierce scuffle lasted for some time. After a while, when all were tired and some were injured, the spoons ended up in the hands of the strongest and quickest. A peace was declared, and all the men sat down on the floor to eat.

Each person could only have so many spoonfuls, and then the spoon would be passed on to the next man. Sometimes, someone would try to sneak an extra spoonful or two. Accompanied by some of the choicest words in the felons' vocabulary, another scuffle would invariably result.

As I sat huddled in my corner, watching all that was happening around me, I found it hard to believe I was actually sitting in this prison. When the meal was over, they brought in some tea that looked more like water. Unexpectedly, one of the prisoners came over to my corner and offered me a lump of sugar. He did not say a single word but made some gesture instead. Apparently, he was dumb and could not speak, but he appeared to be a Jew. He brought some tea for me in a small pitcher and then drank his. This was how I spent my first few hours in prison.

Later that evening, a new prisoner was brought into our cell. He was also a Jew. I hoped his arrival would improve my situation, as I longed for someone with whom I could converse. I went over to him and announced who I was. He was greatly surprised when he heard my name. He had been arrested for setting his house on fire in order to collect the insurance money, so he certainly had troubles of his own to worry about. However, he quickly put his own problems aside and concerned himself with mine.

It turned out that he was a person of some influence. His cousin was a builder-contractor in Kiev and had good connections with the government. Because of this, he was allowed to have food brought into the prison from the outside. He was kind enough to share this food with me. Unfortunately, the following morning my new friend fell ill and was taken to the hospital.

Since my name hadn't yet appeared on the list for rations, I did not receive any bread for the first two days. On the third day, I was finally registered as a regular boarder and began receiving a bread ration, which was the only thing I could bear to eat. I could not touch the soup, because it was served from the bath pails. Once while we were having dinner, one of the men found a quarter of a mouse in the pail. It must have gotten into the soup from the grits that were kept in the prison storage pantry. The man who found the carcass proceeded to make a big fuss and display it to one and all. His goal wasn't to incite a protest against the prison administration, but to cause such a loss of appetite among the prisoners that he would end up with a larger portion for himself.

As the days passed, I found myself weakening and knew I had to begin eating. The only day that I could get food from home was on Sunday, which was visitors' day. I waited impatiently all week for this first Sunday to come. I was especially anxious to receive news about my family. I'll never forget the eagerness with which I looked forward to Sunday. I was so excited that I was unable to sleep that entire Saturday night. All I could do was lie on the floor which served as my bed and toss and turn all night. My back and shoulders ached terribly, and I felt as if I had spent the night on a rake. Since I couldn't sleep, I would rather have gotten up and walked around, but this was forbidden.

At last, the blessed day arrived. On Sunday, a package of food was brought in to me. The parcel was supposed to contain enough food to last for the entire week. When my prison comrades saw the package, they could not contain their joy. They tore it out of my hands in an instant and, in no time, devoured its contents. They fought with one another, each one trying to wrest away a larger share. As they tore at each other like dogs, all I could think about was having to face another week of fasting. Meanwhile, the men in the group constantly kept their eyes on me to see how I was reacting. If I showed any signs of displeasure, my comrades would have given me a beating. So, I put on a happy face and pretended to enjoy watching them eat my food. I was practically forced to say to them, "Eat heartily!"

That autumn was particularly cold. Since almost all of the windowpanes were broken, we froze during the nights. Our suffering was further exacerbated by the condition of the floor, which was wet and filthy and covered by vermin crawling all over the place. My entire body was bitten and scratched.

The month finally passed, and I was transferred to the other quarters. Here, too, there were about forty inmates, most of whom were prison guests of long standing. Fortunately, there were three Jews in this place, and they became my new companions. They made quite a fuss over me when they heard about my case.

I had been transferred to my new quarters on a Saturday. Since the next day would be Sunday, I anxiously awaited the arrival of another package of food. However, I was apprehensive about what would happen to it. My new Jewish friends told me how to handle the situation so I wouldn't be robbed again. They said I should give the package to them and they would look after it. They explained that the other prisoners were afraid of them and would not bother us. When my parcel of food was brought to me, I did as they suggested, and we spent the next five days eating and drinking together. However, since the date of their trial had arrived, they were released.

As long as these other Jews had been with me, the Russians left me alone. As soon as they left, the Russians came over to me. Surprisingly, they treated me rather respectfully. They had heard of my case and were fascinated by the questions the investigator had asked me. They all predicted my worries were for naught. One of these men was especially friendly and was continually showering me with compliments. From the beginning, I couldn't understand his excessive kindness, for he did not seem to be the type of person that had a naturally pleasant disposition. Only later did I discover the real story, and it cost me dearly.

CHAPTER 7

The Bloody Analysis

That next Sunday, I again received a food package. The other prisoners were just as pleased as I was when it was brought in. One of them offered to take charge of it for safekeeping, but I could see right away that he was an unsavory sort of person who could demolish my package in the twinkling of an eye. I thanked him for his gracious offer but refused, explaining that I felt I could take care of it myself.

A little while later, three new prisoners were brought in. One was a Jew, and the other two were Russians. The Jew cried to me that he could not eat the food and he had no sugar for his tea. I offered him some *challah** and sugar, which he gratefully accepted.

He wanted to know what crime I had committed. Since I

---

* A traditional Jewish bread prepared especially for the Sabbath and other holiday meals.

wanted to avoid the usual condolences and expressions of sympathy that people voiced upon hearing who I was, I told him I was in prison for stealing a horse. I asked him what he was charged with. He told me he had paid for a purchase with five hundred rubles he had received. The money turned out to be counterfeit, so he was arrested.

Once, while I was out on the promenade, one of the other prisoners called out my name. This young Jew turned around in amazement.

"You are Beilis?" he shrieked in astonishment. "Why didn't you tell me that in the beginning? Why did you conceal your name? I am honored to be in the same cell with you. Do not grieve, for God will help you."

I was warned that the time was fast approaching when the prisoners were going to "analyze" me. Since I wasn't yet familiar with the prisoners' lingo, I didn't know what this term meant. I soon found out.

When several prisoners are implicated in the same case, it is important for all of them to get together and agree on what they are going to say at the trial. If there is a stranger in the cell, he might overhear their discussions and report to the authorities. It is, therefore, necessary to subject this other prisoner to an "analysis." First, they give him a preliminary beating. If he doesn't report this beating to the authorities and turn the culprits in, then the other prisoners know that this prisoner can be trusted; they feel that they can speak safely and freely in his presence.

Now I began to understand the reason for their friendliness. They pretended to become close with me so that they could pick a quarrel with me and perform the "analysis." It seemed, however, that not all the prisoners were in favor of analyzing me. The one who was angry because of my refusal to make him the guardian of my package undertook the mission. He also had it in for Jews in general, because it was a Jew who had accused him of theft. I knew that this particular prisoner was out to get me, but there was nothing I could do about it.

This is how it happened. I wasn't allowed to wear my own shoes. Instead, I had to wear the prison *sabots*, which were shoes held together with nails. At times, I was so distraught I could only relieve my anxiety by pacing back and forth. In the process, my feet had been torn to shreds by the nails in the shoes. One time, when it was just too painful to continue walking, I sat down on a chair. Seeing an opportunity to provoke a fight, this prisoner came running over and asked me to let him sit down on the chair. Before I could even answer, he hit me so hard that my blood started gushing. Everyone was watching me to see how I would react. The sight of the blood frightened them somewhat, and they brought me some water to wash it off. When I refused to take the water, one of them began shouting.

"Stab him! Do away with him! You can see he is going to squeal."

My young Jewish friend came over to me and begged me to be reasonable. "Wash the blood off," he pleaded. "Soon you'll be transferred to another room, and I'll have to remain here. Then they'll take out their vengeance on me. If you wash yourself off, they'll be appeased. You'd better do it for both of us."

I decided to do as he asked and proceeded to wash myself off. Upon seeing this, some of the other prisoners who had opposed "analyzing" me to begin with turned to the prisoner who had beaten me and began to berate him.

"Jews," they said, "must be tested in another way."

The next morning, when I was out on the promenade, the peasant who had hit me and another Russian were standing next to me. The prison guard saw my swollen eye and asked who had done it. Before I had time to answer, the Russian pointed to the peasant. The *nadsiratiel*, the guard, promptly grabbed hold of the peasant's collar and escorted us to the office. On the way to the prison office, we had to pass several guards. Each of them questioned us as to what had happened, and when they were told, they also gave the peasant a hearty blow. When the last guard we passed was told that the peasant was the culprit, he grabbed him by the collar and threw him down a flight of stairs. I was afraid his head was broken.

When we reached the office, one of the officials asked him, "Why did you hit Beilis?"

"I asked him as a comrade to let me sit on his chair," the shaken peasant responded. "He didn't let me, so I hit him."

"Is that the way to treat your comrade?" the official inquired harshly.

"But he takes our children and drinks their blood," the peasant blurted out defiantly.

"Have you yourself seen him kill children?" the official asked.

"No, but I'm told that he does."

"Well then, take this and this!" he said, accompanying his words with a slap. The official then gave the peasant another good beating.

CHAPTER 8

The Spies

S ince it was impossible for me to remain in the same cell with my sullen peasant friend, I was transferred to another room. Only twelve men lived there, most of whom were petty officials, like policemen and such, who had been guilty of minor offenses. They all regarded me suspiciously. However, one of them, a man by the name of Kozatchenko, was a little more amicable than the others.

After a few days, the warden summoned me into the hall and wanted to know how I was being treated in my new quarters. When I told him things were better here, he left.

I learned that one of the guards in my new room would take letters from the prisoners, deliver them to people on the outside and then bring back the replies. He would do all of this for the price of a few *kopeks*. Since I hadn't received any correspondence from my family, and since Kozatchenko was still behaving congenially, I remarked to him I would like to send them a note.

I wrote the letter to my family and, as a precaution, filled in all the empty spaces so that no one else could add to my words. In the letter, I asked about everyone's welfare. I also wanted to know the reason for their silence and inactivity. Why weren't they doing something to help me? They knew I was innocent. I had not heard anything from anyone, so it seemed as if no one had taken any interest in me. I wrote that I didn't know if I could bear remaining in prison too much longer. I also mentioned that the bearer of this letter should be paid fifty *kopeks* and given a reply to be returned to me.

I gave my letter to the guard, and he brought me an answer. I read it and then tore it up carefully so that no evidence would remain. A few days later, the guard asked whether I wanted to send another letter. I told him I did not.

Kozatchenko's trial was going to take place shortly, so he began preparing to leave. He came over to me whispering.

"Listen to me, Beilis. The whole world knows you are innocent. When I'm released, I'll do what I can for you. The prisoners here have given me some information about the real murderers."

He had his trial and was acquitted, and he subsequently returned to the prison for the night. The next morning, when he was about to be released, I also gave him a letter to give to my wife. I wrote to her that the person who was delivering this letter would tell her news about me.

This happened on a Wednesday. On Friday evening, I was ordered to the prison office. With a terrible sense of foreboding, I entered the office and was met by two prison officials, an inspector and someone else. The inspector spoke first.

"You wrote letters to your family?" he asked bluntly.

At first, I didn't know what to say. Even though I realized that someone must have turned me in, I didn't know who it was. I didn't know if the officials were aware of both of the letters or just one. My immediate thought was that Kozatchenko was the villain, because I had been suspicious of him from the start. I decided he must have been the one who turned the letter over to the officials, perhaps hoping to get into their good graces. I didn't suspect the guard of treachery, especially since he had brought back a reply. I decided not to mention the letter that I had given to the guard since I didn't want to unnecessarily implicate him.

"I sent a letter with Kozatchenko," I finally responded to the inspector.

He then read to me both of the letters, including the one that I had sent via the guard. I now realized a trap had been set for me from the very beginning.* The guard had wanted to get the letters from me so he could deliver them to the officials. Nothing else was said, and I was returned to my cell.

That evening was a Friday night, and all I could think about was the contrast between my misery in that dungeon and the Sabbath that was being enjoyed by pious Jews all over the world who were sitting down to beautiful meals and singing *zemiros*.**

---

* What he did not know was that Ivan Kozatchenko was a secret police agent who had been hired by Tchaplinsky to create enough "circumstantial evidence" to support an indictment. Beilis' note was merely a personal message to his family; however, Kozatchenko would later testify that Beilis had also instructed him to poison adverse witnesses.

** Songs of praise sung on the Sabbath and festivals.

My melancholy musing instantly ended when the door to my room was flung open and a guard ordered me to get my things and come with him.

I gathered my belongings and was taken into a small, bitterly cold room where the temperature was at the freezing point. It took only one glance to see that the room was totally bare. I began begging the guard to at least give me a mattress.

"I'll see about it tomorrow," he answered. "For now, it doesn't matter, because tonight you'll surely die." He left and locked the door.

Trembling from both the cold and fear, I sat down on the icy, wet floor in a state of indescribable suffering. All I could do was wait for the morning to come and hope to survive. I could not get the thought of those letters out of my head. I feared that since the letters had fallen into the hands of the officials, they might also have arrested my wife. In the morning, the deputy warden came to check on me. I pleaded with him to do one of two things. He could either order the stove to be heated so that the room would be warm, or have me shot and put an end to my tortures.

"I don't have the authority to do anything myself," he explained, "but I'll ask for instructions. Wait an hour." In an hour he had me transferred to a small, but warm room.

I waited for Sunday to come. When it finally arrived, no one brought me a package of food. I felt certain that my poor family must have been arrested and thrown into jail. Was it my imagination that the children's voices coming from the prison yard sounded like those of my own little ones? I worried that there was now no one in the whole world who was free and would be able to care for me.

On Monday, the warden himself appeared. I asked him if the letters were the reason why I had not received my food parcel on Sunday. He confirmed that I was being held in strict confinement because of the letters.

"You know," he added, "it is forbidden to do such things. As for your package of food, that isn't our fault. Something must have happened at your home. I'll try to get some information for you."

I took the opportunity to ask him to move another man into the room with me who would be a decent companion. I felt I would go mad from the solitude. He promised to grant my request and departed.

An hour later, two young men were brought into my cell. Each had chains on his hands and feet. They both looked so savage I was sure they were murderers. I would gladly have foregone the pleasure of their company, but I had to put on a pleasant face and conceal my true sentiments.

Another few days passed. One morning, I was given a letter from my wife. She wrote she wasn't well and couldn't come herself. But she did send some money. This cheered me up considerably, and I thanked God they were all home. But why was I still imprisoned? I could only speculate about how long my unjust, undeserved tortures would last. When would there be an end to my misfortunes?

These questions tormented me day and night. I would walk around half out of my mind, wondering whether anyone was willing to take up my cause. Why wasn't anything being done to set me free?

CHAPTER 9

A Taste of Prison Life

One day in January, in 1912, I was summoned to the District Court to receive my indictment. My joy knew no bounds for now I would know what I was being charged with and where I stood.

I was escorted to the District Court wearing shoes so worn they lacked soles and dressed in a brownish red Russian sheepskin. Even though my wife and brother, whom I had not seen for a very long time, were sitting in the courtroom, I wasn't allowed even to talk to them. That morning, prior to leaving for court, I had received a letter from my wife and brother telling me that I should announce in court that I had retained Messrs. Gruzenberg, Grigorovitch-Barsky and Margolin as my lawyers.

Once in court, I was handed the indictment. When I realized what it contained, I was stunned. I was not actually charged with the crime of "ritual murder." I was, however, accused of having murdered Yustchinsky or having been an accomplice with others in his murder. I was charged in accordance with the statute that dealt with premeditated murder. The indictment stated that the death of the victim was caused by bodily torture, that before he was murdered the victim had been subjected to cruel torment. In either case, if convicted, the statute called for a confinement of fifteen to twenty years of *katorga*, imprisonment with hard labor.

Of course, had the investigation been carried out as it should have been and the murder treated as an ordinary crime, this absurd indictment could have been considered just a case of a personal frame-up. It would only have constituted the libeling of an individual. However, since from the beginning the investigation of the case had been undertaken only in order to prove a case of religious ritual murder, it turned out to be an indictment of the entire Jewish people.

I was amazed at Fenenko. He had told me that he was not the one indicting me, yet he was the one who had composed the indictment. As I learned later, he had intended to quash the indictment, since there was no proof whatsoever against me. That is what he himself had said. But the Prosecuting Attorney of the Kiev District Court, together with the notorious Zamislovsky and the whole band of the Black Hundreds, forced Fenenko to draw up an indictment. It should be borne in mind that, in the beginning, Fenenko had not even intended to arrest me. Everything that subsequently happened was the work of the procurator, whose name was Tchaplinsky.

Nevertheless, the higher authorities were still not satisfied with the indictment. It didn't do what they wanted it to, and what it did do, it didn't do well. Not only was the foundation for its premises still too weak to gain a murder conviction, but nowhere in the indictment was there mention of a ritual murder charge. The procurator exerted all of his efforts to have this phrase inserted into the indictment. He wanted it to say that Yustchinsky had been murdered for religious purposes. I was told that Fenenko had been summoned before the Minister of Justice in St. Petersburg several times. He had refused, however, to budge. Finally, Fenenko won on this point. The indictment merely accused me of torture and murder without mention of ritual murder. Heartbroken, I was led back to my dark and dingy cell.

Around this time, my feet swelled and were infested with sores. This condition developed because I had been forced to walk around on snow and ice wearing shoes that had no soles. The skin had split open and blood was oozing out. I couldn't bear the excruciating pain, but those around me had little sympathy for my suffering.

One morning, I asked for the doctor to come in and examine me. I was in agony. The officials were finally merciful and sent me to a *feldscher*, a surgeon's aide. The *feldscher* looked at the sores and said I needed to be transferred to the hospital.

Later, a guard came in. "Hurry up," he shouted. "Let's go."

I could not move. My feet were so swollen that I couldn't even stand up. The guard refused to listen to reason and just kept shouting, "Move on!"

One of the prisoners who happened to be in the hall brought me some rags and wrapped them around my knees. I was thus able to drag myself to the hospital by crawling over the snow and ice on my hands and knees. When I entered the hospital, I was seen by another *feldscher* who had lived on the Yurkovskaya, not far from our factory. When he recognized who I was, he turned pale and trembled with surprise and pity. He ordered that I be undressed at once and given a warm bath. Afterwards, I was given fresh linen and put into a warm, clean bed. I needed rest so desperately I slept for thirty-six hours straight. I just couldn't get out of bed.

After I awoke, the doctor operated on my feet. However, the *feldscher* who was my friend was not present. When the doctor started to open the sores, I screamed from the pain. The doctor just smiled.

"Well, Beilis, now you know for yourself how it feels to be cut up," he smirked. "Now you can imagine how Andriusha must have felt when you were stabbing him and drawing his blood, all for the sake of your religion."

It is impossible to fathom how I felt, lying there and listening to my doctor speak this way. He leisurely continued cutting on my feet, and I had to bite my lips to stifle my screams. After the operation was over, two prisoners carried me to bed where I lay for three days. As a matter of simple decency, I should have been allowed to stay there for a longer period of time, but the doctor was not inclined to make it any easier for me. My old clothes were put back on me, and I was sent back to prison. When I got back to my room, I found that my former companions were no longer there.

The loneliness again began to get to me, so I asked for some companionship. A second prisoner was brought in. At first I feared that he would prove to be a spy like Kozatchenko. However, he turned out to be a very honest peasant. He also was an inveterate smoker. The problem was that smoking was of course forbidden in my room. He felt greatly deprived. There-fore, after a couple of days, he asked to be transferred back to his former quarters, since he could not live without smoking. The warden granted his request, and he was about to go back. However, when the guard came for him, he hesitated.

"No, I have pity on this Jew," he said. "He is a very honest fellow. I like his company, so I'll stay with him."

And so he did. He stayed with me for two weeks, until he was subsequently released from prison. Before departing, he em-braced me and wept.

"I know," he said, "that you are suffering unjustly. Trust in God. He will help you, and you will be released. The Jews are an honest people."

Again, I was left alone. I was so obsessed with the depressing thoughts that preyed on my mind that I was driven to the point of melancholy.

CHAPTER 10

My Attorneys Appear

Eight months had elapsed since that ominous morning when I was first put behind iron bars. Eight dark months had rolled away, and the end of my suffering was nowhere in sight. I didn't even know if anything was being done on my behalf in the outside world or who, if anyone, was planning to defend me.

Just after the indictment, my wife and brother further informed me that immediately after my initial arrest they had retained the services of a lawyer by the name of Margolin to defend me. I was told, however, that I could not see my attorney until after I had received the indictment. Thus it was, on one of those dreary days, that the door of my cell unexpectedly opened and a distinguished gentleman of Jewish appearance entered and introduced himself as Mr. Gruzenberg. He explained that he was one of my attorneys, but he had not been able to see me earlier because of the aforementioned law. Now, however, since the indictment had been completed, he would be able to come to visit me as often as he wished. I was very impressed by his appearance and grateful that he was so supportive.

"Be strong," he said warmly. "I come to you in the name of the Jewish people. You must forgive us, since you are being compelled to suffer for all of us. I tell you that I would be happy to trade places with you and put on your prisoner's clothing and let you go free."

"I have only one request Mr. Gruzenberg," I replied. "I must know what is going on. You must tell me how my case stands. I won't give up hope no matter how bad the news is, but I cannot continue to live in this state of uncertainty. Just tell me the truth."

"You're right," he said. "You ought to know everything, but no one is able to gauge the situation with precision. I had a similar case in Vilna with Blondes, who was also accused of ritual murder.* You can't tell how these cases will turn out."

I repeated to him a Russian proverb that Fenenko had told me during one of my interviews with him. "When the corn is milled, we will have some very fine flour."

"Well, well," said Gruzenberg grimly shaking his head. "We may have *muka* indeed."

This was a clever play on words, since *muka* can mean both flour and trouble. Before leaving, he encouraged me by saying that I was going to be defended by the very best lawyers in all of Russia: Zarudny, Maklakoff, Grigorovitch-Barsky and others. He

---

* In Vilna, in 1900, David Blondes, a young Jewish barber, was accused of wounding his Polish maid in order to obtain her blood to bake *matzah*. Initially convicted, Mr. Gruzenberg helped obtain his ultimate release.

7 7

said that soon I would be visited by each of them.

After his visit, I was greatly relieved. Even though my lawyers had not given me any false hope, I grew more optimistic that I would eventually be released. It cheered me to know there were people taking my interests to heart, to know I had not been forgotten. It was comforting to know that the greatest legal minds in Russia were eager to defend me.

Mr. Grigorovitch-Barsky was the next lawyer who came to visit me.

"Couldn't you have had me released on bail or even appealed to the Czar himself for mercy?" I asked him when he came.

He managed a smile and shook his head. "Do you know that the Czar has recently visited Kiev?"

"Yes," I said. "The newly arrested prisoners told me about it. I also heard that during this visit Prime Minister Stolypin himself was assassinated in the Czar's very presence.* I understand that the chief of the Okhrana, Colonel Kuliabko, the one who originally arrested me, was very upset, since it was his responsibility to prevent such things from happening."

"That's true," confirmed Grigorovitch-Barsky. "So now you know that the Czar was in Kiev. At the time, I was working for the government as an assistant prosecuting attorney. As such, I was a member of the deputation that was selected to welcome the Czar. One of my colleagues who went with me was Tchaplinsky, the Prosecuting Attorney of Kiev. When he was introduced to the

---

* As an architect of the Czar's return to power, P. A. Stolypin presided over much of the government's counter-revolutionary activities, characterizing the tyrannical decadence of the era. A rabid anti-Semite, he was personally responsible for instigating much Jewish suffering.

Czar, he said, 'Your Majesty, I am happy to inform you that the real culprit in Yustchinsky's murder has been discovered. His name is Beilis, and he's a *zhid*.* When the Czar heard these words, he bared his head and made the sign of the cross as an expression of his thanks to God. Now I ask you, Beilis, to whom will you appeal for mercy? To the man who thanks God that a *zhid* is suspected of the murder?"

I was stunned by this response and could hardly recover my senses after hearing this story about the Czar from Mr. Barsky. Everyone knew that Nicholas was not exactly a friend of the Jews, but I was shocked that in front of a gathering of his officials, he would so openly exhibit such an intense interest and pleasure when learning of the persecution of a Jew.

"I'll tell you another thing," Mr. Grigorovitch-Barsky continued in that friendly and winning manner that was uniquely his. "The Czar was scheduled to visit a certain place one day while he was in Kiev, and a great crowd had gathered to greet him. Even though strict order was being maintained, the people were growing restless and quite uncomfortable. I was there with a friend to watch the royal procession. A certain colonel passed by and pushed a Jew, calling him a *zhid*. At the time, my friend and I were dressed in civilian clothes. The Jew who had been pushed by the colonel was nicely dressed and seemed most refined. He certainly had not misbehaved and did not merit the insult. I turned and addressed the colonel.

"'Why were you so rude?' I asked.

"'You *zhid* defender!' He retorted.

---

* A derogatory word for a Jew.

"We had a heated argument, and I eventually brought charges against the colonel. He was subsequently sentenced by a judge to eight days in prison, which was a punishment he certainly deserved for his rudeness. As a result of all these unpleasant incidents, I decided to resign from my position with the government. I gave up my post as the Assistant Prosecuting Attorney and became a private lawyer."

Before Grigorovitch-Barsky had come to visit me, I had been given a paper to sign in which I was officially informed that Schmakov, a lawyer on Yustchinsky's side, was suing me for the amount of seven thousand rubles for civil damages.* Since this lawsuit was related to the murder, it entitled him to participate in the trial against me. During my session with Grigorovitch-Barsky, I asked him who Schmakov was. Grigorovitch-Barsky told me that Schmakov was an old man and an infamous anti-Semite whose opinions were of little consequence. My lawyer seemed rather confident about the prospects for my case. He told me that the greatest experts and scientists in Russia would be summoned for the trial and that, before such a gathering, Schmakov would appear ridiculous. We parted like old friends.

After this, my lawyers visited me regularly. Mr. Margolin was a frequent visitor who also kept in constant touch with my family. He was a tremendous source of solace and reassurance.

---

* In accordance with a unique feature of the Russian judicial system, the victim's family could sue for monetary compensation and hire private attorneys to represent their interests by assisting the prosecution. Even though Mrs. Yustchinsky refused to play an active role in fingering Beilis as the culprit, it was ostensibly on her behalf that such prominent anti-Semites as Schmakov and Zamislovsky participated in the trial.

CHAPTER 11

A Convict with a Heart

Again finding the loneliness intolerable, I asked the authorities for a cellmate. My petition was granted, and a Pole named Pashlovski was brought into my cell. He had been sentenced to *katorga* and was waiting to be sent to Siberia. He was a very resourceful fellow, even if he was a murderer.

One evening, he was summoned to the prison office. Since he had already been convicted, there was no reason for the office to have anything to do with him. I knew it was a bad omen and felt very apprehensive. However, when he returned, he seemed to be in a humorous mood. He came over to me nearly bursting with laughter.

"Why are you laughing?" I asked anxiously. "What happened in the office?"

"Beilis," the prisoner answered, "I would tell you, but you are too nervous. If I told you the whole story, you would become much too excited, so it is better for you not to know."

I renewed my interrogation. "I see you are a good man since you are so mindful of my health. And I thank you for that. But you came in laughing. Otherwise, I wouldn't have known anything was going on. So since you are my friend, you must tell me everything. It is better for me to know the truth, even if it is unpleasant."

He thought about it for a while and apparently decided to divulge his secret.

"Well, if you insist," Pashlovski began, "I'll tell you what happened. I was brought into the office, where many people were gathered. The Prosecuting Attorney, the Warden and the others were all having a lively discussion. The Prosecuting Attorney took a silver cigarette box from the table and offered me a cigarette. You can imagine my amazement. Look who they are, and yet they were treating me, a convict, to cigarettes. I am nobody's fool. Obviously, they wanted me to do something for them. The Warden began speaking earnestly to me in a very sincere, concerned manner. He spoke as if his own life was on the line.

"'You are a Christian,' the Warden said. 'You are one of us, and I am certain you care for your fellow Christians. You are just as worried about the shedding of Christian blood as we are.' The Warden hesitated for a moment and then continued. 'You are in the same cell with Beilis. Tell me, what does he say? Has he told you anything?'

"My answer was simple. 'He is bewailing his bitter misfortunes,' I said. 'He complains that he is suffering unjustly and undeservedly.'

"The Prosecuting Attorney chimed in with a smile. 'We know that's what he says. That's to be expected. But you are an intelligent man who understands people. You can discern the difference between his truths and his lies. Didn't he ever slip up and say something else?'

"I understood at once that this was a devious group, so I made myself quite clear.

"'Look here, gentlemen,' I said. 'I grew up among Jews. At the age of six, I lost my father and my mother. I was an absolute orphan. My relatives apprenticed me to a Jewish locksmith, and I learned his trade. I lived in his house for over twelve years. By the time I left, I was a grown man with a trade, able to make money and get married. I had friends among the Jews and also among Jewish converts. I daresay that I know all the Jewish customs and a good deal about their religious rites. I know it all from A to Z. This is to be expected since I grew up in a Jewish house as one of them. I know they wouldn't eat an egg if it had a blood clot in it, because this would not be kosher. They cannot eat it. If I have seen it once, I have seen it a hundred times. I've also watched them salt their meat. When I asked the mistress of the house why they do it, she said that this draws out all the blood from the meat, since they are not allowed to eat any blood whatsoever. Now when people come and tell me the Jews use blood, human blood, when they tell me that Beilis has murdered a Christian child to use his blood, I, as a Christian who believes in the cross, can tell you that all these stories are a set of despicable lies.'

"When I was through with my say, they all looked at me with murder in their eyes. They saw they had the wrong man. They realized that the cigarette was of no avail, and some of them lost their patience.

"'Well,' said the Prosecuting Attorney, 'be that as it may, surely he says something in his sleep.'

"I said I had never heard you talking in your sleep. They finally understood they weren't going to get very much out of me, so they ordered me back to the cell. That's why I was laughing when I returned to the room. Don't you see? They don't have any proof against you. They're looking for yesterday's snow!"

They didn't allow Pashlovski to stay with me for very long. They noticed that he was too affable towards me, so they took him away. Since they couldn't utilize him for their purposes, they split us up. As a result of episodes such as this, I was convinced that the government knew its case was weak. It was clear to me that had the Black Hundreds felt their case to be stronger, they would not need the help of spies and convicts.

CHAPTER 12

New Intrigues

R umors had circulated in the prison that a journalist by the name of Brazul-Brushkofsky* had written to the Prosecuting Attorney that he had certain information indicating that Vera Tchebiriak's lover was the one who had committed the murder of Andriusha Yustchinsky. It was further rumored, however, that even though Brazul's story was based on Tchebiriak's own admission, there was not enough corroborating evidence to support his contention. Evidently, a new investigation launched in the spring of 1912 was on the right track, and Brazul-

---

* A member of a respected Russian Orthodox family and a major contributor to the largest liberal newspaper in Kiev, Brazul-Brushkofsky, later joined by the renown criminal investigator Krassovsky, bravely embarked on an undercover mission that entailed befriending Vera Tchebiriak and her cohorts. It is largely due to his efforts that the true facts surrounding the murder are known. Tragically, he suffered persecution and imprisonment as punishment for his role in aiding Beilis.

Brushkofsky, aided by a friend named Krassovsky, disclosed the additional information. As a result of this, the first indictment was set aside, another one was drawn up, and Vera Tchebiriak was subsequently arrested. When I heard about all this, my hopes soared. However, my optimism was short-lived. That summer, a new District Attorney was sent down from St. Petersburg, provoking yet another upheaval in the investigative process.

A day or two after the incident with Pashlovski, I was summoned to the District Court. I went joyfully, for I was happy to see the outside world again and breathe fresh air. This time, my escort took me in the tramcar. As ill luck would have it, the car caught fire, and we had to go the rest of the way on foot. Many people knew I was going to be taken down to the Court, and some came just to get a look at me and take my photograph. I was led into a hall where District Attorney Mashkevitch and a certain professor were waiting for me.

"Look here, Beilis," Mashkevitch said. "Three hairs were found on Andriusha's trousers. If you don't object, I would like you to give me some of your hair so I can show it to an expert."

I was so startled by the request, I could scarcely look at the man, but I answered politely, "If you need it, you can take it."

"No," said the District Attorney. "You must do it yourself."

I took the scissors from his desk, cut off some of my hairs and put them in an envelope. Later, I began to regret what I had done. Who knows what tricks these people might be up to? They might dye the hair or something. I calmed myself when I figured out they could do whatever they wanted, even without my help. Since, for the time being, my hair was all they wanted, I was immediately sent back to jail under armed guard.

Three days later, I was again ordered to the prison office. This time they wanted my fingerprints.*

"Is this done in every prisoner's case?" I asked.

"No," I was answered. "But it is required in those cases where the indictment calls for *katorga*."

"What is it for?" I inquired further.

I was told that fingerprints were found on Andriusha's belt-buckle. My fingerprints had been wanted in order to compare the two. Once the imprint of my fingers was obtained, I was dispatched back to the cell.

At about this time, my wife was given permission to come and see me in prison. "To see" is about all that she was able to do. The visit only lasted five minutes, and we were separated by double bars. We tried to speak, but there was so much noise and tumult in the visiting quarters, we could hardly hear each other. Nevertheless, seeing her brought me much joy.

One day, I was given the good news that my wife and children were being allowed to visit me in the prison office. I was escorted there forthwith, but when I entered, my family was nowhere to be seen. I sat down to wait patiently, but soon I became restless. I had not seen my children for a very long time, and I wondered how they were. I could only imagine how much they must have suffered. And for what? The minutes seemed longer than the years. The wait was interminable.

---

* It is interesting to note the degree of modern forensic technology available at this time. The prosecution intended to employ a similar level of technological sophistication to "scientifically" prove the existence of mystical Jewish blood rituals.

The six officials who sat in the office were watching me the entire time, exchanging remarks among themselves. District Attorney Mashkevitch was one of them.

Finally, my wife, the children and my brother were brought in. My wife's sister was not allowed to come. When I saw my youngest son, who was four years old, I took him in my arms and began to kiss him. A guard rushed forward and snatched the child away from me. He said I was not permitted to kiss my child.

My little boy began to weep. He had been frightened by the rudeness of the guard, the presence of the officials with their polished buttons and, most of all, by the way I was dressed. I lost my self-control and began to cry out, with tears in my voice.

"What right do you have to do this?" I pleaded. "Have you no children yourselves? Don't you know a father's feelings? Are you so heartless?"

I noticed that several of the officials turned their faces away and were wiping their eyes with their handkerchiefs. I was permitted to take the child into my arms. I asked my wife how things were going with her.

"Even if I have enough to live on," she answered sadly, "what good is it when you are suffering so cruelly and unjustly?"

We were able to spend a few minutes together, and then, my family was told they must leave. I remained alone. Tchaplinsky, the Prosecuting Attorney, came over to me and offered me a cigarette. In a voice full of "compassion," he began to speak to me.

"Yes, Beilis, this is how your Jewish friends are acting," he said. "When the Jews needed you, they gave you money and told you how loyal you were. And now, when they don't need you anymore, they forget all about you. Your poor wife is also suffering terribly. She, too, must be very angry at the Jews."

Tchaplinsky had spoken very slowly and distinctly, and he had assumed a tone full of friendly sympathy. His every word, however, was like a stab in my heart, and the cunning, malicious expression on his face only added to my bitterness. I turned to him and asked for permission to say a few words.

"Certainly," he said.

"If an atrocious villain could be hired to murder an innocent child," I said, "and if, because of this murder, the mobs would be incited to carry out a pogrom and kill many Jews, do you think the Jews would have a part in it? Why would the Jews want to cause a pogrom? Let me be kept in prison. I have become a patient man. The trial will show that I am innocent."

None of them said another word to me, and Tchaplinsky turned away. He obviously was not satisfied with what I had said. I was led out of the office.

My imprisonment had lasted for over a year. Four hundred days had elapsed since that fateful morning when I was first arrested by Colonel Kuliabko and torn away from my wife and family. For a long time, I kept hoping that "tomorrow I will be free." Instead of freedom, I had to content myself with hopes and expectations.

One evening, while I was sitting in my dingy cell alone with my thoughts, I heard footsteps and several voices in the hallway. A woman was speaking outside my door.

"I am curious to see this rascal," she said.

The door opened, and four persons entered. One of them was wearing a general's uniform. The woman looked at me and said in a horrified tone, "What an atrocious creature! How fierce he looks!"

The general came closer to me and said, "Beilis, you will soon be set free."

"On what grounds?" I asked him.

He replied. "The three hundredth year anniversary of the reign of the Romanov dynasty is soon to be celebrated. There will be a manifesto pardoning all *katorjniks*."

"That manifesto," I said, "will be for *katorjniks*, not for me. I don't need a manifesto. I need a fair trial."

"If you are ordered to be released, you will have to go," the general persisted.

"No. Even if you open the doors of prison and threaten to shoot me, I will not leave. I will not go without an opportunity to prove my innocence. I am strong enough to endure this suffering until my trial."

While I was speaking, they had all stood quietly, listening attentively to my every word. Even that persnickety lady, who had been so frightened by my appearance and had thought that I looked so cruel, came closer to get a better look. When I finished, the general continued in the same vein.

"Listen to reason, Beilis," he implored. "You know very well that you are suffering unjustly. I would probably do the same thing if I were in your place. You were a poor man, and you did what you were told. If you tell us the truth, you would be making a very smart move. You would be sent abroad and taken care of for the rest of your life. By cooperating with us, you would provide an answer to the question that has captured the attention of the whole world. However, by remaining silent, you are continuing to conceal the truth. Do you think you are protecting the Jewish nation and only ruining yourself? Why should you suffer for nothing? It is your decision, but if you would just talk, you could be happy for the rest of your life."

I could hardly contain myself while the general was speaking. I was disgusted by his every word. He had actually come to give me some advice. He must have sincerely believed he was expressing sympathy for my situation. According to him, I had been hired by the Jews to do this piece of dirty work, and now, he wanted me to tell "the truth." He came to try and exert some influence over me. I saw that any further discussion would be useless. I couldn't stand it any longer. My answer to him was short.

"You're right," I said. "The whole world is waiting for the truth, and the real truth will come out during my trial."

"Well, we shall see," the general muttered. Waving his hand as if hopelessly giving up, he left my room with his companion.

The first year of my imprisonment had drawn to a close. I found it hard to believe that I had subsisted for so long in such a place. During the frosty winter, the heating in my prison cell was so poor that the cement plastered walls were coated with ice. During the warmer days, the lime on the walls would thaw, causing the walls to drip with moisture. The trickling from the ceiling made it almost impossible for me to sleep.

I had to wear the usual prison garb, which consisted of a long coat of ragged cloth and a sack-linen shirt that had to be worn for stretches of two to three months. In the prison itself, the mortality rate from typhoid fever alone was about six or seven men per day. This was not surprising at all, considering the unbelievable filth, the disgusting food and the unheated rooms. There was also no lack of the usual *cooties*.* At times, it was so cold I would awake to find my hand frozen to the ice on the wall. All of these factors created a perfect breeding ground for various diseases and epidemics.

The door of my cell was sealed shut with no less than thirteen locks. This meant that each time the door was opened, all thirteen locks had to be released. The sound of the rasping springs used to set my nerves on edge. My mental state had so deteriorated that I was obsessed with the illusion that somebody behind me was hitting me repeatedly on the head. It was one blow after another.

In addition to these hardships, I was tormented by frequent searches conducted by the officials. The searches were usually performed by a squad of five under the supervision of one of the deputy wardens. Every time they would come in, the first order was for me to undress. Often they had to unbutton my clothes themselves, because my fingers were too stiff from the cold to perform this simple task. They were quite rude and usually tore off a number of buttons during this operation. Some took this opportunity to display their "sense of humor."

"You liked to stab the boy Andriusha and draw his blood. We will do the same thing to you now."

That was the standing joke, but I never knew if they were serious. They would also look into my mouth to see if I had something hidden there. They would pull my tongue out to see deeper and better. I had to undergo all these tortures and insults

---

* Slang for lice.

six times a day. It is hard to believe, but it's the truth. Protests were useless. They intended to harass me as much as possible. They wanted me to die without having to actually murder me. They would not poison me outright, for that would create trouble. I believe they wanted to drive me to suicide. Cases of suicide were quite frequent in the prison. Prisoners would hang themselves to escape the persecution and torture. The administration must have thought I would succumb to the abuse. They presumed I would not be able to tolerate such treatment and would take my own life. If this occurred, then the charge of ritual murder against the Jewish people would never be disproved. The authorities could depend on the Black Hundreds to circulate the rumor that my "suicide" had been caused by my fear of a trial, rather than any remorse for the murder I had committed.

My life was thus hanging by a hair. I once saw another prisoner shot to death in the prison hallway because of an altercation with one of the guards. This murder was easily explained away. The guard tore one of his sleeves and reported that he had shot the prisoner in self-defense.

There was no punishment, of course, for such "self-defense" was deemed justifiable. On one of the walls of my cell there hung a set of prison rules. One of its clauses stated that a prisoner who was insubordinate or assaulted a guard could be shot on the spot. The term "assault" required no special definition, nor was the term "insubordinate" any more specific. If a guard ordered the prisoner to walk more quickly or to stop and wait, and the guard was not instantly obeyed, the guard could claim that this constituted resistance and insubordination, thus warranting an execution of the prisoner. Incredibly, the guard even received a reward in the amount of three rubles for this noble act.

Generally speaking, the life of a prisoner in jail is hell. From the very moment the prison gates are closed behind him, a prisoner is completely under the command of the administration, and his life is in constant danger. Nevertheless, in spite of the danger and all the abuse heaped upon me, or perhaps because of it, I was more determined than ever to go through with this great trial. I knew that the administration was just looking for some excuse or pretext to do away with me, so I was always on my guard and accommodated them in every possible way.

More than once, there were incidents of foul play where they intentionally attempted to provoke me. They tried to make me resist or act in an insubordinate manner. They often strove to put me in a situation where they could resort to force against me. But I was extremely careful. I always kept in mind that the honor of the Jewish people must be protected and that the shameful charge of ritual murder must be erased. It was my fate that the responsibility for this fell in my lap. And the only way I could fulfill this responsibility was by remaining alive. It took every ounce of my strength to suffer silently, but I could not allow the enemies of my people to triumph.

CHAPTER 13

Between Hope and Despair

The days were dragging along. When was my trial going to take place? There were periods when I felt perilously close to going insane. At such times, I would stare at my guard in amazement. I would think to myself, Is this really happening to me? Am I the man lying here on this cold and filthy floor, among these creeping creatures? Is this the same Mendel Beilis who used to be a man of consequence, dressed like other human beings, who used to live a peaceful life with his wife and children?

I experienced mental tortures that are hardly possible to bear, much less describe. Lack of exercise and constant worry deprived me of sleep. When on occasion I did manage to fall asleep, I was troubled by the wildest nightmares, which exhausted me more than the sleep refreshed me. Usually in my nightmare, I was either being led to my execution or pursued or choked and beaten. I would awaken trembling with fear and breathless from having tried to escape from my imaginary persecutors. I would experience a sort of relief upon awakening to realize I was still in jail, in my prison cell, and not in the torture chamber of my dreams.

The nervous strain was depriving me of all my strength, and I feared I would soon relent. I sought consolation in the knowledge that the day of my trial was speedily approaching. Surely, the day of my trial would come and the world would recognize the truth. My innocence would be proclaimed, and the Jewish people would remain untarnished by terrible calamities such as this that have been perpetrated upon them by their detractors. The world would know that Jews do not murder gentiles, nor do they draw their blood.

However, the date for my trial had not yet been scheduled. The officers of the courts were still undecided about what to do. First, I was told that the trial would take place in March. Then it was postponed until April. Nothing was definite. What was the problem? Why were they so slow?

The reason for the delay was really quite clear. The indict-ment had already been drawn up, and those who were most interested in pressing charges against me were not satisfied with it. Fenenko, the *Sliedovatiel*, had told me himself that he had not wanted to indict me because the material gathered during the investigation did not provide him with enough grounds to support a prosecution, much less pursue a charge of ritual murder.

The procurator, however, was more stubborn. He was determined to make a case against me at all costs. A Jew had to be imprisoned so that this case would be remembered for generations to come. This is why they continued to push for an indictment, even though there was no foundation to support it.

In the year 1913, in the beginning of May, the indictment was formally presented to the Superior Court of the Province of Kiev for endorsement. The Court put the case on its calendar. This triggered a new period of despair for me. If my case was to be tried as an ordinary criminal murder case, then there was a total lack of proof or evidence upon which to base an accusation against me personally. If it were to be treated as a simple murder, the evidence should have compelled the authorities to arrest Vera Tchebiriak with her gang of thieves and to press charges against them. However, since the Czar himself had expressed the desire that a Jew be prosecuted, and since the higher officials naturally wanted to humor him, they were forced to suspend the normal laws that would have applied and proceed against a Jew. And this Jew was me. But if the case was to be based on a charge of ritual murder, then why didn't they state that accusation in the indictment? Thus, none of the parties interested in prosecuting me was satisfied with the indictment. I was neither "fish nor fowl," neither a ritual murderer nor a plain murderer. The Czar could not be pleased. Apparently, the Jews had won the first round.

After many long and hair-splitting arguments and discussions, the day of the trial was finally set. It would commence at the end of May. I have already explained that the indictment accused the murderer of Andriusha of malice aforethought since the victim was "grievously tortured." The indictment further mentioned that "two Jews dressed in unusual garb came to

Beilis" and that the Jews were seen to perform their prayers. It also stated that "each year Beilis baked *matzahs* for Passover." Other "crimes" of a similar nature were also enumerated.

My lawyers were preparing for all possible eventualities and insisted to the court that the testimony of experts and scientists was necessary for the trial. Among others, they requested the presence of Professors Kokovtzeff, Tikhomiroff and Troyitzky, all professors of theology or of Hebrew language in the higher academies for clergymen. They also subpoenaed the former procurator of the Holy Synod, Prince Obolensky, and Herman Struck of the theological faculty of the University of Berlin as witnesses.

One day, while I was sitting in my cell thinking about my forthcoming trial, I heard a noise in the hall indicating that the many locks to my door were in the process of being opened. The clang of the thirteen locks kept reverberating until, finally, the door flew open. I expected to see the spiteful faces of my guards, but it was Mr. Grigorovitch-Barsky instead who was being ushered in. With his usual kindness and cordiality, he calmed me considerably and asked how I was being treated by the administration.

Then he came to the point of his visit. "Mr. Beilis, rumor has it that, in spite of the indictment presented to you, it looks as if the whole trial will never take place."

"Why?" I asked, perturbed as much as amazed.

"It's simple," he replied. "There is just too much proof against the real murderers. New facts have been brought to the attention of both the public and the officials by a Russian journalist, Mr. Brazul-Brushkofsky, who has diligently devoted himself to the case. He has collected new material and presented it to Colonel Ivanoff of the Okhrana. The evidence gathered by Brazul-Brushkofsky is so important that the investigation is likely to be reopened, and in all probability, your indictment will be quashed. Of course, it will be a bitter pill for your persecutors to swallow, and they will put up a fight, but it looks as if they will have to give in."

My joy was so great that I began to weep.

"Don't cry, Mr. Beilis," Mr. Barsky said softly, himself quite moved. "I completely understand your situation. Rest assured that you will eventually be released. Of course, it's impossible to predict how long they will drag it out. You can see for yourself that they are trying their best to grasp at straws, but we feel very hopeful their efforts will come to naught. If not now, then sooner or later, they will have to release you."

Mr. Barsky bid me farewell, expressing the hope that he would soon visit me as a free man, enjoying the company of my family. I was jubilant. The whole indictment against me was falling apart.

Even though the real murderers had finally been uncovered, I figured that the investigation would still have to take some time. If all of those who had been so involved in trying to prosecute me had instead busied themselves with trying to find the real perpetrators of Yustchinsky's murder, it would have been so simple. All they had to do was get hold of Vera Tchebiriak and her gang. It certainly would have taken a lot less energy to have prosecuted them than try and build a case against me. Vera and her cohorts had been arrested at the very beginning of the investigation, even before I was, but their imprisonment was not what the "higher-ups" really wanted to accomplish.

But that was in the past. Now, in spite of everything, the truth was going to come out after all! Even the Black Hundreds would realize that I had innocently been thrown into the dungeon and that I ought to be released.

I was delirious with joy, eagerly awaiting my approaching liberation. I practically forgot all that I had suffered over the past year. I conjured up images of what that morning would be like when the guards would come and proclaim, "Beilis, you are free! You can go home. You are innocent."

The new developments that had been related by Mr. Barsky threw me into a state of anxious restlessness. Every time I heard footsteps in the hall, I felt certain that an official was coming to announce my release. Several days passed in this manner, days of strain and impatience. Seeing that my hopes were not being realized, I began to have doubts. Who knows whether the information was based on solid facts? Perhaps my lawyers simply wanted to cheer me up. Maybe the case had taken such a bad turn that they felt the need to give me some false hope in order to strengthen and sustain me for the bitterness of what lay ahead.

I did not, however, want to believe any of this. From Mr. Barsky's previous visits, I always had the impression that he was a frank and sincere person. I did not think that he would conceal anything from me. Even if the news was truly terrible, he would tell me the truth. And since he told me that there was a chance for my speedy liberation, how could I doubt his word, especially since we both knew how completely innocent I was?

The days were lapsing, then the weeks and the months, and there was still no change in my situation. I understood that new circumstances must have arisen, but whether they were for the better or for the worse, I did not know. Above all, I was afraid of Colonel Ivanoff's name, for he was a colonel and a gendarme. In my opinion, this was not a good omen. The man was not likely to do anything in my favor. His duty, of course, was to please the higher officials, not to alleviate my suffering.

For a while, things were quiet, and no one came to visit me. I was neither summoned for the trial nor was I told to go free.

CHAPTER 14

More Interrogations

I was summoned several times to the *Sliedovatiel*. He was Mr. Mashkevitch, the notorious anti-Semite, whom I have already mentioned. Once during the interrogation, he said, "Tell me, Beilis, did your father ever go to see *tzaddikim?*"

I was dumfounded by this question, since I had expected him to announce my freedom. He was apparently starting the interrogation all over again. What new tricks did he have up his sleeve? Had not the interrogation process ended? It seemed to me that the prosecutors only had two choices—to try me or to release me. But once more, it was the same old story, with *chassidim* and *tzaddikim*. Weren't the authorities carrying this point a little too far? I told him I could not remember. If it had happened, it had taken place years ago.

"Are you a *chassid* or a *misnaged?*" he continued to ask.

"I am a Jew," I replied. "And I don't know the difference

between these two groups. We are all Jews."

"Do you know whether Zaitzev ever went to a rabbi?"

"I don't know."

"Are you not related to the family of Baal Shem Tov*?"

"Mr. *Sliedovatiel*, I have no idea."

"Do you pray with a *tallis*** or without a *tallis?*"

I had answered this question once before. I had explained that before my marriage I had prayed without a *tallis* and after my marriage I prayed with the *tallis*.

"What do you need the *tallis* for?"

"I don't know what it's for."***

"Now, Beilis, tell me," the *Sliedovatiel* droned on. "What is it exactly that you call an *afikoman?*"

Again, it was the same absurd line of questioning, the same foolish questions with which the first *Sliedovatiel* had confronted me over a year ago. I figured that maybe the new man just wanted to find out whether Fenenko had investigated the case properly and that once he had the information he would release me. After all, Fenenko himself had asked me these foolish questions, and hadn't he ultimately admitted that he had no evidence against me?

I wasn't able to explain properly to the *Sliedovatiel* what the

---

* Eighteenth century founder and charismatic leader of *chassidus*.

** A large white shawl traditionally worn by Jewish men during prayer.

*** It must be remembered that Beilis had been forced to live most of his life apart from the Jewish community, thus effectively depriving him of a formal religious education. In his youth, he was conscripted into the army of the Czar, and as an adult, he had spent fifteen years as the only Jew living at the factory. In spite of these circumstances and his lack of knowledge, he steadfastly maintained his Jewishness.

afikoman was. During my childhood, I had lived in a village. Then, I was taken to serve in the army for several years, so I didn't have much of an opportunity to learn about the religious rites in depth. I know that I used to eat *matzah* and that the *afikoman* was actually a piece of *matzah*, but I did not know any more about it. And even had I known, it would have been difficult for me to explain. He had more questions.

"Do you have a brother that is a rabbi or a *shochet**?"

"No, we don't have any rabbis in the family. If there were any, over fifty or a hundred years ago, I am not aware of it. There might have been a rabbi or a *shochet* at that time. However, not now."

He was silent for a minute or two and looked as if he wished to remind himself of something. Several times, he leafed through some papers in front of him. At last, he asked another question.

"Do you have any connection to Schneur Zalman Schneyerson, the well-known Rabbi of Liadi**?"

"No," was my answer. "I have a good friend by that name. He lives in Kiev and often came to visit me, but I do not know the Schneyerson family in Liadi, and I am in no way related to it."

With these, and similar questions, he kept plying me for about two hours. Then he started to read from a book written by a scientist named Pronaitis, who was trying to prove, with all sorts of sophistry and misquotations from the Torah and the Talmud, that the Jews actually use blood for their *matzahs* and

---

* One who slaughters permitted animals according to Jewish law.

** The founder of Chabad *chassidism*. In 1813, his son, Rabbi Dov Ber, moved from Liadi to Lubavich. The prosecutioner felt the case against Mendel Beilis would be strengthened if he could be connected to a *chassidic* group.

that the blood was baked into the *afikoman*. The *Sliedovatiel* also mentioned the names of Schmakov, Professor Sikorsky and Golubov, who were also supposed to know all about Jewish religious rites.

I am sure that during the interrogation, he must have felt that he was exhibiting a great deal of knowledge about our Torah. His questions, however, provoked a burning anger in me. It was he who was drawing my blood with every question that he asked. I was his prisoner. He had total control over me, and he could do whatever he liked. I was, however, helpless, and I had to answer him.

The grilling itself would not have produced such a painful reaction from me had I not noticed the manner in which he treated my answers. I could see, from his smirk and his negative response to my answers, that all these questions were superfluous. As far as he was concerned, the case was crystal clear. He felt quite certain that the Jews needed blood for Passover and that the blood was put into the *afikoman*. He believed beyond a shadow of a doubt that all of this could be substantiated by scientists such as Pronaitis, Schmakov and Sikorsky.

By the time the inquisition had ended, I realized that my indictment would not be quashed. I knew I would have to stand trial. However, I could not understand why there had been the need to interrogate me yet again since the indictment itself had already been completed. Presently, this too would become clear.

CHAPTER 15

Attorneys under Attack

I spent the summer in a state of total uncertainty. The autumn brought no changes, and winter was approaching. During all these months, no one visited me, and I had no idea of what was happening outside the prison walls. For a long time, all I had wanted was to have the trial take place as soon as possible so I could prove my innocence to the world. Then, after Mr. Barsky had told me the charges against me were baseless and that the case was invalid, I expected the indictment to be quashed.

These hopes were dashed when I realized that another investigation had been started all over again. Apparently, events had taken a new turn, yet I was kept in the dark. Even though it had now been several months since Mashkevitch had concluded his interrogations, I still had no idea what was going on.

I was informed later, by one of my lawyers, that Mr.

Grigorovitch-Barsky had been telling me the honest truth at the time of his visit. All my lawyers had been of the opinion that the whole case would be dismissed and the trial would never take place.

As I have already mentioned, the journalist Brazul-Brushkovsky, together with a police captain named Krassovsky, had undertaken in earnest to discover who the real murderers were and to gather the necessary evidence. With this in mind, they made the acquaintance of Vera Tchebiriak and her gang, visiting her several times and interviewing her neighbors. They collected a considerable amount of material and presented it to Colonel Ivanoff.

Colonel Ivanoff ordered a careful investigation to verify Brushkovsky's contentions. As a result of his efforts, the Colonel came to the conclusion that Yustchinsky's murder was the work of Tchebiriak's criminal band. Ivanoff conducted his investigations in the strictest secrecy and when he finished, he sent the material to the Prosecutor of the Superior Court.

At first, the Prosecutor's office showed no interest in the Colonel's reports. Although these reports came from an official source, and from no less than a member of the political Secret Police, the Prosecutor ignored them. Nothing would have come of it had my attorneys not taken a determined stand. When my lawyers learned that these new facts had been discovered, they demanded that the preliminary investigation be reopened. This happened in the spring of 1912.

The higher judicial authorities and the Black Hundreds were most upset by this turn of events. They naturally feared that a new investigation based on Brushkovsky's discoveries would result in the disclosure of the true criminals. This was what they feared most. Yet, they could not openly go against the letter of the law. Whenever new evidence appeared, the law required a new investigation.

They were not happy with Fenenko, and they did not want him handling this new investigation. They felt that he was too "soft." He was, therefore, given a leave of absence. He was simply removed from my case. Thus, Tchaplinsky was ordered to come to Petrograd to act as the Prosecuting Attorney for my trial and to confer with Shtcheglovitoff, the Minister of Justice. He was also to meet with the heads of the Black Hundreds.

There was, at this time, a group of officials in the Ministry of Justice who were inclined to have my case quashed just to "get out of the slimy bog." That attitude prevailed during a certain period of time, and it was then that Grigorovitch-Barsky announced to me the "good news."

In the end, however, the Black Hundreds prevailed. They insisted that if a new investigation was to take place, it had to be done "right." If there was going to be another investigation, then they would see to it that a new indictment would result and that this new indictment would contain the charge of ritual murder.

The final decision was indicative of the level of corruption that Shtcheglovitoff had brought into the Ministry of Justice. Not only did they agree to have a new investigation, but they even arranged to have the indictment written first. This way they could make sure that the investigation produced enough "evidence" to support a charge of ritual murder. Thus, they arranged for an investigation to be undertaken just for the sake of appearances.

Mashkevitch was put in charge of the investigation. He was

not concerned with the fine points. With him, it was all very simple. He was looking for *chassidim*, *tzaddikim*, rabbis, white robes; in short, all the paraphernalia that should appear in a ritual murder case. It was to be a production that could have appeared in one of the books written by the fathers of the Inquisition.

For the sake of appearances, the materials gathered by Brushkovsky were also examined, but instead of sending them to the prosecutor, as was the rule, they were first dispatched to the Ministry in Petersburg and then sent back with proper comments and annotations.

As I was told, the authorities were unable to find in the Procurator's Office in Kiev a man capable of formulating the type of indictment they wanted, one with "teeth in it." Finally, a suitable person was found. Even at that, the indictment was not prepared at once. It was turned inside out and doctored up several times. The work was done by the Assistant Prosecuting Attorney, Count Rozvadovsky. When it was ready, it was forwarded to the Superior Court of Kiev for approval.

The enemies of our people were still not satisfied with their work. They now started to go after those who only sought the truth.

The Chief of the Secret Police of Kiev was a man by the name of Mishtchuk. He and two of his detectives, Smalovick and Klein, were prosecuted for having been "partial" in their investigation of me, since they had leaned towards my side. Mishtchuk was found guilty and received a year of imprisonment. He was also deprived of his civil rights. The two detectives were similarly punished.

The police captain Krassovsky, who had a record of twenty years of service with the police department, was charged with having embezzled the amount of seventy-five kopeks, which equalled about forty cents. This sounded like a joke in comparison to the millions of rubles that are routinely involved in the bribery of higher officials. The case against Krassovsky was dismissed.

Vera Tchebiriak proceeded to file criminal libel charges against the journalist Brushkovsky. The same thing happened to the well-known journalist, S. Yablonovsky. Of course, Vera Tchebiriak didn't do this on her own. She was directed to do so by those above.

It was the Black Hundreds who turned their attention towards my lawyer Margolin. First of all, he had published a book detailing the absurdity of the ritual murder charge. The Prosecutor claimed that Mr. Margolin was thus trying to influence the inhabitants of Kiev, from among whom the jury would eventually be selected for the trial. The second charge was that he had attempted to bribe Vera Tchebiriak in order to persuade her to assume the guilt of Yustchinsky's murder. She alleged that he had offered to pay her forty thousand dollars if she would agree to "confess."

A similar charge was filed against Mr. Barsky, since he had signed a public paper protesting the ritual murder charge. He received a reprimand from the court. His subsequent appeal was lost in a higher court.

Hearing of all these events, I could see that my case had indeed taken an unfavorable turn. I felt that a tightly woven net was about to entangle me. My lawyers tried to keep my hopes up and encourage me. They assured me that in spite of all these machinations the truth would finally prevail. Taking their words to heart, I prepared myself to wait for the long postponed trial.

The Attempt to Poison Me

Spring had arrived, yet I was deprived of the opportunity to witness the awakening of nature that was granted to all God's other creatures. All were merry and free. All that is, except me.

It was the third year of my confinement in that dark cell where I could not even move about. For over two years, I had barely seen my family. I had to wallow in filth and breathe the sordid, damp air of the jail, scarcely ever seeing the sun that shines upon the righteous and sinners alike. The rays of light could hardly penetrate my prison window. However, I still felt a little better, for during springtime it was not so cold in my room, and the mild breeze coming through the gratings refreshed me.

On one of these days, I received a visit from Mr. Grigorovich-Barsky. After we exchanged the usual pleasantries, he told me that he had a request.

I wondered what it could be. I asked. "What could you possibly want from me?"

"I want you to do something. It will be hard, but you must do it."

"What is it?"

"You must stop receiving food from home."

"If you say so," was my answer. "I will do whatever you tell me. I guess you know what you're doing, but could you at least tell me why?"

"Yes, of course," he responded. "I'm asking you to do this because the Black Hundreds have been writing in the newspapers lately that the Jews are attempting to poison you. They are spreading the story that the Jews are afraid you might slip up and say a wrong word and confess your guilt. Because of this, we are afraid that the Black Hundreds might arrange your poisoning so that the case will not be tried and they won't have to fear losing face in front of the whole world. If you die now without a chance for us to defend the Jewish people, they think people will still believe that their accusations are true. That must be their intention.

"Therefore, we have decided that the best thing you can do is not accept any more food packages from home. That is the only way to stop these hooligans and their insinuations. If you do not receive any food from outside the prison, they will not be able to claim that the Jews are trying to poison you. And it will deny them an opportunity to poison you and blame it on the Jews. We know it will be very hard for you, but there is no other way."

Of course, I promised him I would do as he asked. Later, as I was thinking the matter over, I felt that if the Black Hundreds wanted me poisoned they could just do it themselves. It would be so easy for them to get one of the prison guards to do it. Therefore, I petitioned the warden to permit me to get my food myself from the common kettle. The usual procedure was for a prison guard to bring my food to me in my cell. When I was first imprisoned and sharing a room with a large number of men, enough food for ten or twelve people was put in one large bowl. I was not afraid that they would put poison in such a large bowl, for then they would have had to poison the whole crowd in order to get rid of me. But now that I was all alone in a cell by myself and they passed me my food through an opening in the door, I did not feel so safe.

At first, my petition was refused. The official response was, "If you want to eat, eat what you are given. If not, you can starve. There will be no special privileges for you. Don't worry. We shall not poison you. It is your Jews that you should fear. They are not satisfied with using our blood and are inventing additional lies to make us appear ridiculous."

I had good reason to be stubborn. So I declared a hunger strike. Three days had elapsed. Whenever a prisoner doesn't eat for a few days, the Prosecutor is summoned to investigate. The Prosecutor finally appeared. I told him I wanted to get my food myself from the kettle and not to have it brought into my room.

His reply was that it could not be permitted. "You must not leave your cell. You are supposed to be under strict confinement. The other prisoners and guards are not even allowed to look at you."

"Well," I answered, "then let them turn away when I draw my ration."

Somewhat to my surprise, after considerable bickering and arguing, I was allowed to get my food from the common kettle. I was again reduced to subsisting on that starvation diet, since I was no longer receiving any food from home and the prison broth was unfit to eat.

CHAPTER 17

A Murderer's Suicide

At about that time, I heard a very interesting story, which I expected to be of great use to me. However, it proved to be a disappointment. Here is a short account of it.

When the new evidence collected by the journalist Brushkovsky was being examined, the authorities arrested Tchebiriak's thieving friends, Rudzinsky, Singayevsky and Latischeff. They were arrested upon altogether different charges.

One day, Latischeff, who was the principal murderer, was summoned by Fenenko, who was still the *Sliedovatiel* then. Fenenko commenced to ask his prisoners questions relating to my case. He mentioned that, according to some fresh evidence, Latischeff and the other members of the gang had been implicated in Andriusha's murder. According to this new information, Tchebiriak was the primary culprit who had ordered her three accomplices to do it. Fenenko gave such specific and detailed information that Latischeff thought Fenenko surely knew the whole truth.

After the interrogation had lasted for about an hour, a confession was drawn up for Latischeff to sign. And he actually did so. Apparently, he was so flustered and confused by the questioning that he didn't fully realize what he was doing. Later, however, he must have regretted that he had signed the confession so hastily and implicated himself. Apparently, he made a move for the desk in order to destroy both the confession and his signature, but his escort was on the alert and prevented him from snatching the document. This alone was sufficient proof that Latischeff was somehow involved in Andriusha's murder.

Three days later, he was again summoned before the *Sliedovatiel*. Fenenko began to ask him more questions about the crime, and this time the questions were hitting so close to home that Latischeff found it impossible to keep his story straight without contradicting himself. The *Sliedovatiel* began to write down these additional confessions. Latischeff noticed a carafe of water standing on the window sill and asked for permission to take a drink. He leisurely approached the open window and had a drink. He then jumped out of the window, falling a full four stories to his death.

The reasons for his suicide were quite simple. He was the archmurderer and leader of the gang. When he saw that the truth was finally known, he realized he would have to spend the rest of his life in prison. He, therefore, decided to put an end to his life.

His suicide caused a considerable stir. However, as incredible as it may seem, it was not allowed to affect the course of my case.

This was because the new *Sliedovatiel* understood better than Fenenko that the most important thing was not to catch the true murderer. He knew that his job was to please the Black Hundreds and the higher officials. The other two murderers, Rudzinsky and Singayevsky, were released shortly thereafter.

CHAPTER 18

The New Indictment

I was again called to the prison office. I found the *Sliedovatiel Mashkevitch* sitting at his desk, quite at ease. He appeared to be in the best of moods. After muttering some hasty response to my greeting, he picked up a thick document from his desk and handed it to me.

"This is your indictment," he said with an air of self-importance.

I stood there speechless and did not know what to think. The first indictment had been relatively short, consisting of five pages. This one was practically a book. It was about thirty pages long. I did not expect anything good to come of this.

I was so dejected I could barely walk back to my cell. Still reeling from apprehension and confusion, I must have been walking rather slowly. My guards decided to quicken my step with a couple of blows. Once I reached my cell, I lay down upon my cot and could not even raise my head, much less read the indictment. I just stared at the papers. So, I thought, this is the sum total of my life and my crimes. They had written so much and yet I was an innocent man, who had never hurt a fly in his life. I was being kept a prisoner while the actual murderers were free, strolling the streets, protected by what was called "Russian justice."

And so the die was cast. They could not find anyone else, so the lot had fallen on me. They had been searching and investigating, and at the upper levels a decision had finally been made. Mendel Beilis must be tried and convicted.

Well, let the trial take place, I sighed to myself. At least the whole world will see what atrocious villainies are being committed in the Holy Czarist Russia. I crawled off the bed clutching the indictment to see what these people were charging me with. I had to strain my eyes in order to see the small letters. My eyesight had been affected by the darkness of the cell, so I could only read it in bits and pieces. What were they seeking and what had they found?

At first, it looked quite simple. When the autopsy on the murdered boy's body was performed, a number of wounds were observed on various parts of the body. There were thirteen wounds on the throat, on the skull and around the ears. In all, thirty-seven wounds were discovered on the whole body.

Professor Obolensky of Kiev University and his assistant had performed the autopsy and an analysis. They came to the conclusion that the wounds on the neck and the skull had been inflicted while the victim was still alive and the heart was still strong. As the heart became weaker, the other wounds were inflicted on the body. Thus, the first stabs were those that were on the throat and the head, and the last ones were those that were near the heart. These experts were also of the opinion that the stab to the heart was inflicted by pushing a knife all the way up to its hilt, which could be seen by measuring the depth of the wound. Their conclusion was that the murderer deliberately tortured the child.

Professor Kosorotoff, whose opinion was also sought, confirmed the findings of his colleagues. He added that the murder could have been perpetrated by one or more murderers. He was also of the opinion that it was the intention of the murderer to torture the child.*

This was the expert opinion concerning the murder itself. If they wanted to find the motive for the murder, they would have to find the culpable party. At this point, the indictment related one wild story after another. After reading these accounts, it was possible to discern the basis for the whole frame-up.

The indictment stated that at the beginning of the investigation it was learned that on March 12, at six o'clock in the morning, Andriusha had left his house for school. Later, it was discovered that he had not attended school on that day and had not returned home.

---

* A first autopsy, performed on March 22, found no evidence of a ritual murder, so a second autopsy was performed on March 26. Its conclusion, still inadequate, was "revised" on April 25 after a "conference" with Tchaplinsky. With the death of its primary author, this "scientific" testimony of Professor Kosorotoff was needed to confirm the "findings." After the trial, receipts were found showing that Kosorotoff was paid the large sum of 4,000 rubles for his "travel expenses."

At first, his mother thought he had gone to spend the night with a relative named Natalie Yustchinska. The next morning, the mother discovered that the relatives had not seen the boy, and a search for him began. The search lasted for several days until, finally, his dead body was found. In the beginning, the indict-ment continued, there were rumors that his mother had showed little interest in the fate of her son. Moreover, when his body was found, she was alleged not to have manifested any motherly feelings. She did not weep nor seem to be particularly disturbed. Because of all this, she was arrested, and the police searched her house. After several days of detention, the authorities reached the conclusion that not only were the rumors unfounded but they were the baseless inventions of her enemies.

At about the same time, rumors began to circulate that the Jews had murdered Andriusha. The indictment stated that the authorities had not attached much importance to those rumors because they were still under the impression that Andriusha's mother was involved in the murder. Four witnesses had ap-peared, declaring that the boy's mother had not displayed any signs of mourning when the body was discovered. They even added that a day or two after the disappearance of the boy, his mother, with the assistance of another man, was seen dragging something enclosed in a heavy bag.

The investigators also pursued another lead that was sup-posed to connect them to other people who might have perpe-trated the crime. It was as a result of this that the thieves Rudzinsky, Singayevsky and Latischeff were implicated. There had been rumors to the effect that Andriusha had uncovered the secrets of this band and that they had threatened to harm him if he ever betrayed them. Therefore, there was a possibility that they were the ones who had done away with him. Tchebiriak had also been suspected, since Andriusha had often been seen in her house.

In reading all of this, I felt somewhat relieved. Thus far, the investigation seemed to be on the right track. I began to hope the indictment would not be so terrible after all. In reading further, however, I began to see a complete change in the narrative.

All of this had taken place in the beginning. That is, these were the opinions that the investigators initially expressed. But later, all of this gave way to a new version. According to the indictment, this phase of the investigation was brought to a close. They concluded that these "gentlemen," namely Singayevsky and Rudzinsky, who, by the way, were notorious murderers and thieves in the neighborhood, were simply paragons of virtue. Tchebiriak was similarly held in high esteem. She was seen to be the "purest of the pure." Earlier in the document, the honor of Yustchinsky's mother was also cleansed. How could such an accusation be leveled against so "perfect a mother"?

In short, the indictment concluded that all the prior suspects were decent, honest people and simply should not have been charged with such an abominable crime.

The real culprit, according to the indictment, was a Jew named Mendel Beilis, the manager of Zaitzev's brick factory. It was I who was selected for the role of Yustchinsky's murderer. I had been living on the factory grounds for a number of years without ever having hurt or molested anybody. But it really did not matter, for supposedly I had not murdered Andriusha for personal reasons, such as for robbery or the like. According to the indictment, I had murdered him for religious purposes. Ironically, the indictment continued, crimes of this nature required a "*tzaddik* or a rabbi" or a "good Jew," thus my integrity worked against me. I, of course, was no *tzaddik*, but the indictment alleged that I was. A number of queer stories were invented to make me appear the murderer.

At the time, continued the indictment, when the journalist Brushkovsky uncovered new facts and turned them over to Colonel Ivanoff, suspicion had turned again to Tchebiriak. One of her neighbors, a Russian woman named Molietzky who lived in the lower story of the same house, had even stated in a deposition that on the day of Andriusha's disappearance she had heard a child's screams coming from the apartment occupied by Tchebiriak.

But such evil things couldn't be said about Tchebiriak. Who could believe it? Why, hadn't she herself told the story of what Brushkovsky had done to her, how he had taken her on a trip to Kharkov for a conference with an "important person"? And hadn't that person offered Tchebiriak forty thousand dollars if only she would take upon herself the guilt of the murder? This "important person" was said to be none other than my lawyer Mr. Arnold Margolin. Tchebiriak "affirmed" that this was all true and further stated that of course she had indignantly rejected the tempting offer because she could not be bought with money. Hence it was clearer than daylight, the indictment surmised, that Tchebiriak was virtuous and innocent and a totally credible witness.

Equally clear was the policy of the authorities. All the thieves and villains were similarly whitewashed. It was the journalist

Brushkovsky and Captain Krassovsky who were not to be believed, even though prior to this whole episode they had possessed spotless reputations.

In order to make the charges against me plausible, it was necessary to make the crime a ritual one. Hence, it became imperative to base the charges upon the expert opinion of learned Christians who could declare positively that the Jews used blood for Passover.

I could not read any further. My nerves were shattered, and I passed out exhausted on my cot. In the morning, I again began to read further.

Just what was the expert opinion of these scientists? The indictment spelled it out very clearly. Yustchinsky had been murdered in a very unusual manner. As soon as his body was discovered, rumors had begun to circulate that the Jews had committed the crime for religious purposes. The investigative authorities were therefore justified in asking for an expert opinion in order to clarify the situation. For this information, they turned to Professor Sikorsky of Kiev University, to the professors at the Theological Academy in Kiev, to professors of similar subjects in the Academy of Petrograd, including Troyitzky and Glagoliev, and finally to the person who was "renowned" as the "Master of Religious Sciences," the Reverend Pronaitis.

The question put to Professor Sikorsky probably cannot be equalled in all of legal history. He was asked whether it was possible to determine the nationality of the murderer from the evidence, and if he could express an opinion on what motives had prompted the murderer to commit the crime.

Although it was a most astonishing question, this "great"

scientist, who was a Professor of Psychiatry and himself somewhat unbalanced, was not abashed by it. He responded that the crime had been deliberately committed by a Jew and it had been done for the purposes of racial vengeance, to "avenge the Children of Israel." The professor further testified that the murder had been well-planned and could not have been carried out by an insane person. He added that the murderers had not gone straight for the heart, because their aim was not to accelerate the death but to achieve their special ends, which was to draw out blood and torture the victim.

The professor divided the crime into three distinct phases: the drawing of the blood, the inflicting of torture and the actual murder. That, he explained, was why Andriusha had been stabbed so many times. The professor concluded that the deed was committed by one who was "experienced in that kind of work." Such was Sikorsky's opinion.*

As obviously ludicrous as all of this "expert" testimony appeared to be, the authorities accepted it as valid. Two other professors who were the most prominent Russian authorities on the Bible and Talmud, Glagoliev and Troyitzky, were asked questions about Jewish laws and rites. Glagoliev answered that there does not exist in Jewish literature any law or custom allowing Jews to use blood in general or Christian blood in particular, especially for religious purposes. He further stated that the prohibition against shedding human blood or using any blood whatsoever was to be found in the Bible and, insofar as he

---

* There had been an outpouring of Russian as well as international criticism of Sikorsky's report. To prevent any further damage to the government's position, some medical institutions were closed and the press heavily censored.

knew, was never retracted or abolished in any later writings. He did not find any specific prohibition to that effect in the Talmud or in the rabbinical laws.

Professor Troyitzky was also quoted as having said that the Jews were forbidden by their religious laws to use blood. He also stated that they were strictly forbidden to murder any human being, whether Jew or non-Jew. He did add that the expressions "A gentile studying the Torah is subject to death" and "Murder the good among the gentiles" are to be found in the Talmud, but he finds them difficult to explain. He knows of no proper explanation.

In summing up, these professors testified that both the Torah and the Talmud prohibited Jews from using any blood, human or not. Regarding *Kabbalah*, he was unable to express any opinion. He was unacquainted with the *Kabbalistic* literature, and he did not know what, if anything, was said in those texts about the usage of blood.

Then the indictment proceeded to turn to the leading Christian expert on *Kabbalah*,* the ex-Catholic priest Pronaitis. This was an interesting development. Glagoliev and Troyitzky, who were distinguished professors at the highest theological academies and considered the greatest Russian authorities on Jewish subjects, expressed an opinion that helped my case. They explicitly stated that the Jews were forbidden to use any blood, especially human blood. It would therefore seem that there could be no "ritual murder" charge, since no such ritual existed. But if there were no ritual, then all of the accusations that had been

---

* Jewish mysticism.

leveled against me would fall to the ground. And this, of course, the authorities could not allow. So they sought the answer in the *Kabbalah*. They searched high and low among professional clergymen, but they could not find anyone bold enough to say that he possessed any knowledge of this area of Jewish theology.

Finally, a priest by the name of Pronaitis, whose name had heretofore been totally unknown, declared that he was conversant in Talmud as well as *Kabbalistic* literature. This great master of *Kabbalah* gave, as his expert opinion, the following: All the Jewish rabbis, as well as Jews in general, are united in their hatred of the Christians. A gentile is considered a "beast harmful to man." Thus, he could explain the prohibition against murder. This prohibition, according to Pronaitis, referred to the Jews alone, for only they were considered human. It did not refer to Christians, who were considered animals.

Having done with the Talmud, the learned priest then turned to the *Kabbalah*. He held that the murder had to be committed in a specific manner as prescribed by the *Kabbalah* and that blood played an essential role in Jewish ritual. It was used as a remedy for many diseases. He stated that when blood was needed it was not necessary to slit the victim's throat. The blood could be drawn out by stabbing the victim. According to this priest, the opinion that the Jews were actually forbidden to use blood was mistaken. Even the Talmud likened blood to water and milk, he said.

Pronaitis then proceeded to enumerate a number of "scientists" and swindlers like himself, quoting their opinions in regard to the question at hand. He placed particular emphasis on the verdict of a certain apostate who had formerly been a rabbi and was now a priest. Pronaitis declared that this person said that Jews could eat cooked blood. This renegade was further alleged to have stated that Christian blood was good for eye diseases. Such was the information that Pronaitis, in the name of the renegade, gave to the court.

It is curious to note that even the renegade never claimed that he had any personal experience in these matters. He demurred that it had been his father who had shared this information with him and that he had taken a son's oath never to divulge the secret. While the renegade had been a Jew, he had kept the details confidential. But now that he had changed his religion, apparently he wanted to share this knowledge with the world.

As if all this rigmarole were not enough, the indictment went on to discuss certain "evidence" that had been given by various people that would tie me to the crime. Tchebiriak's son Zhenia was alleged to have testified that he had seen "strange Jews," *tzaddikim*, in my house. It was not possible to determine whether or not Zhenia had actually said such things, because he had died in the interim. However, his nine-year-old sister corroborated his story. They professed that they had once gone to the Beilis house to buy milk and had looked through the window and seen two strange looking Jews in funny hats and black robes. The children said that they had become frightened and had run away.

Furthermore, on the day of Yustchinsky's disappearance, the girl said that she had been playing with some other children in the factory yard when Beilis started to chase them away. They all ran and climbed over a fence to safety, but she claimed that she hid because she wanted to see what Beilis would do. She testified that she saw Beilis and the two other Jews catch Andriusha

129

Yustchinsky and drag him into the house.

Among other stories, there was also included a report of the incident that had happened in prison involving the letter I had smuggled to my family through Kozatchenko. The spy Kozatchenko had quite a lively imagination. He testified that once he had gained my confidence he persuaded me to write a letter. Not only did I write the letter, he recounted, but I shared with him many secrets. He related that I asked him to do a job for me once he was out of prison. He claimed I offered him a great deal of money to poison two incriminating witnesses. The arrangements were that certain Jews would provide him with the poison, as well as a deposit of fifty rubles. I supposedly promised him that the Jewish people would greatly reward him and support him for the rest of his life if he could successfully accomplish the mission.

All this testimony resulted in the conclusion that I, in conspiracy with some unknown men who had yet to be discovered, had committed a premeditated murder of a Christian child for religious purposes. We had taken Yustchinsky, gagged his mouth, inflicted thirty-seven wounds on his head, neck and other parts of his body and had then drawn out his blood.

It was already March when I had received this second indictment. Pacing in my cell, I would often take out that document, most inappropriately called a Court Indictment, and re-read it again and again till the blood would almost freeze in my veins. I was helpless. The whole of Black Russia, with Czar Nicholas at its head, was against me.

When I was presented with the second indictment, I was asked once more whom I was retaining as my lawyer. I answered that I wished to retain my former attorney. Shortly thereafter, I was visited by Mr. Barsky. He informed me that Mr. Margolin had been forced to withdraw from the defense, because the Prosecuting Attorney had summoned him as a witness. The law forbade someone to be both a witness and a lawyer in the same case.

Mr. Barsky also told me that, besides him and Gruzenberg, I would also be defended by Messrs. Maklakov and Karabchevsky. When Mr. Barsky came for another visit, we spoke about the case. He would always encourage me to be brave and strong. He felt certain that the truth would surface, like oil in water, and that the Black Hundreds and the anti-Semites would suffer an ignominious defeat. He also advised me to ask the Prosecuting Attorney for a second copy of the indictment. He explained that I had the right to request another copy and that I should inform the officials that my lawyers needed a copy. I, therefore, dispatched a petition to the Prosecuting Attorney requesting a second copy.

The next morning, Mashkevitch came to the prison.

"Do you really wish to have a copy of the whole preliminary investigation?" he inquired.

"Yes, I must have it."

"If you insist, then you will have it, but I must tell you that it may make things worse for you. It may delay the date of the trial for another few months."

I asked why Fenenko had been able to give me a copy without any problem.

He laughed at me. "You are foolish. Fenenko was a child. He believed all the stories you told him. Don't compare me to

Fenenko. He had drawn up a worthless indictment , while I made one that came straight to the point. Anyhow, if you wish to have the trial delayed, you may have another copy."

I was in a desperate dilemma. If I did not get another copy, then my lawyers would not be able to make a thorough study of the indictment in time. They would be unable to prepare their pleas or get to the very heart of the prosecution's arguments. Were I, on the other hand, to get a copy, then the date for the trial would be postponed. It had been so difficult to wait thus far that I could not envision waiting any longer. There was a chance that Mashkevitch was just trying to frighten me, but then again, maybe he was telling the truth. If he wanted to put any obstacles in my way, he was certainly able to do so. Clearly, it was his policy to make me suffer as much as possible.

After considering the matter, I decided not to ask for a copy. I believed that my lawyers could manage without it. Perhaps they knew of another way to obtain a copy. Surely, they had more avenues of getting one than through a helpless prisoner. At least, I would not cause the trial to be delayed any further.

A few days later, I was told that my wife and brother were waiting in the Warden's office. This rendezvous was my only consolation during this entire period of my imprisonment.

I entered the office and saw my wife and brother sitting there. Mashkevitch was also present. I began to ask them about the family. One of the questions my brother asked was, "Have you received a copy of the indictment?"

I told him I had been informed that the trial would be delayed for another few months if I were to procure that copy and that I had therefore decided not to get it.

"You mustn't listen to all their excuses!" my brother shouted. "Get a copy and don't pay any attention to their stories."

The Warden had been present throughout our entire conversation, and he jumped to his feet, bellowing, "Get out of here at once. What impudence!"

It was a long time before the Warden regained his composure. He kept pacing the floor, mumbling, "What insolence, what impudence." He also promptly ordered my wife to leave. After this episode, I expected to hear that my brother had been arrested. I spent several sleepless nights worrying about it.

A few days later, my wife again came for a visit. This time we met in the prison office, so we could only talk through a double grating. She was able, however, to tell me that my brother had not been arrested.

It was with the greatest impatience that I awaited that much longed-for trial. Two and a half years had elapsed since that fateful day when the chief of the Kiev Okhrana, Kuliabko, had arrested me at my house. Meanwhile, Kuliabko's fortunes had plummeted. The well-known revolutionist and half-traitor Bogrov had managed to penetrate the theater when Czar Nicholas had come to visit Kiev. It was there that Bogrov had assassinated Prime Minister Stolypin in the presence of the Czar. Kuliabko's career thus came to an abrupt and disastrous end. It did not, however, improve my situation in the least.*

---

* When it was discovered that Bogrov's father was of "Jewish extraction," thousands of Jews fled and prepared for a pogrom. It was postponed so as not to further disrupt the Czar's visit. However, it was at this time, in September of 1911, that it was decided to appoint a new prosecutor and pursue the blood libel "frame-up" with more vigor.

Now, at last, the great day was approaching, the day that not only I and my family but the whole Jewish nation had breathlessly awaited all these years. Nay, the whole world, even many gentiles were anxiously waiting for it, for all wished to know the truth. They all wanted to know how the Russian people would decide my fate as well as the fate of the Jewish people.

I was aware that I was being defended by the most erudite lawyers in all Russia. I also knew that there were many enlightened, humane compatriots on my side.* But what good would this do me when the Russian justice system was controlled by the government and its puppets? It was impossible to predict any outcome or even to know what might happen next. All I could do was hope that the bubble of lies would burst.

---

* Many of the leading men from all areas of Russian society had bravely and publicly protested this obvious travesty of justice. They were not just defending Beilis or the Jews. They were defending the honor of Russia and the integrity of her judicial systems in the eyes of the world. Tragically, most paid dearly for their open criticism of the Czar.

CHAPTER 19

The Trial at Last

As hard as it was to have spent over two years in prison not knowing exactly what I was being accused of, it was even harder to await the day when I would be put on the dock before the judges, when the whole conspiracy would at last unfold. But, as the proverb says, as long as we live, we live to see.

One day, I finally received the formal summons to appear for trial on the 25th of September.* That was still over two months away, but at last, the shore was in sight. With each passing day, the end was coming closer. Another few days and it would all be over.

---

* Unbeknownst to Beilis, the government intentionally postponed the proceedings in order to exploit the situation and continue to incite anti-Jewish feelings among the masses. At one point, Beilis was imprisoned an additional year and a half so that reactionary, anti-Semitic candidates could defeat Jewish and liberal opponents in a Duma election.

My mood was one of joyous optimism. I tried to envision what it would be like—the various procedures of the trial, the reading of the indictment, the questions I would be asked, my answers. All my thoughts concentrated on the approaching trial. I could not think of anything else.

About two weeks before the trial, I began to petition the authorities for permission to wear my own clothes that had been taken away from me when I was brought into jail and forced to exchange my clothes for those of a prisoner. I submitted this request because I was embarrassed to appear in such a public arena so shamefully attired.

However, I did not receive an answer to this request. Two or three days before the trial, I was again visited by my wife and brother. The tears flowed freely, of course. We expressed the hope that before too long we would be in our own home, free and unmolested.

Before she left, my wife told me that I would be permitted to wear my own clothes and that they would be issued to me that very day. The next morning, the thirteen locks of my cell began to click, signaling that the door was being opened. Usually, this process filled me with apprehension and fear. This time, it seemed to have a different sound. The clicking was more encouraging, as if bringing good news.

"Well," said the guard. "Here are your clothes. You can dress yourself. Your trial begins today."

I was taken into another room where I was given the suit of clothing that had been taken from me two and a half years earlier. I was only too happy to discard those ugly prisoner's clothes and to put on my own. I was too afraid to savor the thought that I might never have to put those filthy rags back on ever again, so I just gratefully enjoyed this opportunity to be able to look like a human being.

That day, the authorities treated me with friendliness and respect. As if by magic, all their former viciousness disappeared. Some of them even helped me get dressed. I could not imagine such politeness on their part after all the suffering to which they had subjected me. When I was ready, I was handed over to the escort squad. They even behaved differently. The command was given: "Forward march!"

As we came out of the prison yard, a pleasant sight confronted me. Each time I had previously been taken to the Prosecuting Attorney, there had been no one in the yard except for a few guards. This time, the yard was packed, as if there was going to be a great military review. The regular army was there, as well as all the administrative officials. Everyone, from the lowest guard to the Warden himself, had come out to watch me leave. I was the center of attention. Some smiled under their moustaches, but the majority were stiff and serious. Besides these, several hundred Cossacks with glistening lances were stationed in the yard. Their unsheathed sabres were an indication that they had come to protect me from an "evil eye." I was seated in a black armored prison coach, surrounded by an entire array of officials and accompanied by the army cavalry. It was in the midst of all this pomp and grandeur that I was escorted down the road to the Court of Justice.

From the window of my coach, I could see that the streets were lined with people who were not deterred by the less than propitious weather. The dark and foreboding clouds seem to imply that the heavens did not view the whole spectacle very favorably. The crowds, however, did not seem to mind. The Black Hundreds, who could be distinguished by their badges, were present in large numbers. I could see their ugly features, popping up at every turn of the road. On the pavements, in the windows and even on the roofs of the houses, I could see multitudes of people.

As I progressed along the way, I noticed the faces of Jewish men and women, some wringing their hands and wiping their tears with their handkerchiefs. I did my share of crying as well.

To insure order, and also probably to watch me, a line of Cossacks on horseback was positioned the full length of the road from the prison to the courthouse, a distance of about two miles. Passing through the cordon, we finally reached the District Court House which was surrounded by thousands of people. The gates of the courtyard swung open, and our coach drove in.

Alighting from the cab, I said to the driver with a smile, "I'll pay you on my way back."

The Chief of Police and a police captain who were standing nearby could not refrain from chuckling.

Once inside the courthouse, I was led into a separate room, the special place prisoners were assigned during their trials. I restlessly waited to be led into the courtroom. I had been anticipating this day for so long that, now that it was here, I could hardly believe it wasn't all a dream.

All the months and years seemed to pass before my eyes— Kuliabko dragging me away from my family, the Okhrana, the District Attorney, the tzaddikim, the afikoman, the prison, the days of hunger, the nights of sleeplessness, the guards, the swollen feet, the operation, the surgeon cutting endlessly and mercilessly, Fenenko, Mashkevitch, the General and that lady, all those endless tortures.

My God, when was it all going to end?

CHAPTER 20

Karabchevsky

The door of the chamber opened, and a distinguished, athletic-looking man with a flowing mane of hair came in and greeted me. I was startled, as if awakening from a bad dream, and looked at that handsome, friendly, smiling face.

"Good morning, Mr. Beilis. Don't be alarmed. My name is Karabchevsky, and I am your lawyer."

I had known that he was to be one of my lawyers at the trial, but I had seen only Messrs. Grigorovitch-Barsky, Gruzenberg, Zarudny and Margolin. They often came to visit me in the prison. Until the trial, I had never met the other two, Messrs. Maklakoff and Karabchevsky.

The sudden appearance of Karabchevsky made a strong impression on me. It was as if a beam of light had penetrated the room. His friendly greeting and cheerful tone not only freed me from the nightmare of my thoughts, it also made me feel as if I was to be released at once from my very imprisonment.

The famous advocate came closer and said, "Be of good cheer, Mr. Beilis. Keep up your courage. I would be happy to come closer to you and shake your hand, but unfortunately, an exceptional rule has been declared in your case, and no one, not even your lawyer, is allowed to come within four steps of you. If I were to violate this ruling, I would be severely reprimanded. So tell me, how do you feel? How have you been?"

His cordial and friendly words had such a strong effect on me that I forgot I was a prisoner. I felt as if I were a free man surrounded by friends. However, all it took was one look at my escorts, who were ceaselessly watching my every movement, to make me realize I was still very much in their clutches.

I began feeling hungry, and also, I wanted to smoke. I mentioned this to Karabchevsky.

"Is there any way I can have something to eat, or perhaps smoke a cigarette? I will starve if I am to wait for food to be brought to me from the prison. I have some money to buy food from the court restaurant."

While I was speaking, the colonel who was in charge of the guards who escorted me came into the room.

Karabchevsky turned to the colonel and asked, "Why isn't this man allowed to smoke?"

The colonel responded sharply, "Because prisoners are not allowed to smoke."

"That may be," Mr. Karabchevsky replied, "but right now this man is not in prison. Besides that, he must be given something to eat. The trial is about to begin, and it will be long and arduous. He will need every bit of his strength. It is a serious matter, and I implore you to grant Mr. Beilis these two requests. If you do not, even though it may not even be in your power to do so, I will nevertheless feel compelled to complain publicly at his trial of his mistreatment. A man like Mr. Beilis certainly should not be subjected to such ordeals."

Mr. Karabchevsky's words made quite an impression on the colonel. He realized instantly that he was no longer dealing with Beilis the Jew but with Karabchevsky, the distinguished Russian lawyer. Karabchevsky's threat to make the issue a public one must have been taken seriously, for the colonel asked to be given a few minutes to consult with his superiors. Apparently, the problem was not a simple one, and he could not assume responsibility for handling it alone.

As the colonel turned to leave the room, he quietly called over the guard. "Go ahead and let him smoke," he said.

Pulling a three-ruble bill out of his pocket, Karabchevsky then went over to the soldier and said, "Here, take this and go find him some cigarettes."

A few minutes later, the soldier returned with some excellent cigarettes. Karabchevsky was very pleased that he had been able to procure for me so quickly both the privilege and the pleasure of enjoying a smoke. It helped put my mind at ease.

When the Colonel returned, he announced that the appropriate authorities had decided to allow me to purchase some food from the restaurant located in the courthouse.

"Well, Mr. Beilis," my lawyer said with a genuine sense of accomplishment, "if there is anything else you need or want, all you have to do is tell your lawyers about it. We will certainly do everything we can to help you. All you have to do is not give up.

After all, your fate is not totally controlled by those who have imprisoned you. You are in the hands of God, and in ours. My colleagues and I are eager to get on with this trial. Of course, we pray to God that such trials don't have to take place in Russia, so that our beloved country could be spared the shame, but since we have to go through with it, I want you to know that we are honored to play a part in exposing the falsity of these ludicrous charges against you. You will see for yourself. The truth will emerge victorious. I have to leave for a little while, but we'll be together again shortly. *Dasvedania*!*"

Karabchevsky's inspiring words, coming as they did from such a sincere and noble person, filled me with strength and confidence. With renewed faith, I fervently believed in a speedy salvation.

After this incident, the attitude of the soldiers who were guarding me also changed perceptibly, and they became extremely helpful and pleasant. They had never seen a common prisoner treated with such civility. And hadn't the lawyer implied that I wasn't a prisoner at all? They had never heard of anything like this before. What with the guard getting a three-ruble tip and the colonel being sent out to get restaurant food, they realized that this was a unique situation, and they responded accordingly.

A soldier brought me some food from the restaurant. From then on, before he would go to the restaurant to bring me a meal, he would first politely ask what dish I would prefer. Since we were paying good money for it, he wanted to make sure that I received the most appetizing and nourishing food available. I found it

---

* The Russian word meaning good-bye.

impossible to believe that a prison soldier was behaving towards me in such a courteous manner.

I began to feel considerably better. For one thing, for the first time in many, many months, I had a really good glass of tea. This, and the decent food, made me feel much stronger. However, it was still too early to celebrate. Even though those hellish days of suffering and waiting were behind me, the terrible ordeal of my trial still lay ahead. And beyond that, I dared not even imagine.

It must be said, however, that for a prisoner who had been secluded from the world of the living for so many long and weary months, even an hour of ease and pleasure is a great good fortune in itself.

While I was relishing my reverie, the door opened and the colonel announced, "Bring the prisoner into the Courtroom! The trial is about to begin."

I repeated this last phrase over and over again.

CHAPTER 21

The Trial Begins

I was ushered into the main courtroom and told to sit in the defendant's dock. Soldiers stood on both sides of me with their swords drawn, but I paid no attention to them. They were just doing their duty and did not frighten me. This was the day I had longed for, the day when the veil of mystery would finally be lifted and the world could see that the case against me was a baseless lie perpetrated by the evil Black Hundreds who were dedicated to my destruction.

The courtroom on the opening day of my trial was a sight to behold. There were several thousand spectators, from many different stations in life, from various countries around the world. The ladies were resplendent in the latest fashions, while the pompous generals and prominent officials were similarly bedecked, in dazzling uniforms impressively decorated.

What impressed me the most was the array of international

newspaper correspondents who had come from all over the world to cover my trial. The District Attorney, the Prosecuting Attorney and other sundry officials were standing off to the side, engaged in heated conversation, while the judges, who were seated on the dais in the middle of the room, were preparing to begin.

All these people seemed like participants in a play, who had come either to satisfy their curiosity or perform their role. But whether observers or actors, they all focused their attention on me the moment I entered the courtroom. My seat became center stage.

I was most interested in the jury, those twelve men in whose hands my fate actually lay. They had the power to decide whether I would live or die, be imprisoned or freed. I took one look and my heart sank. My first impression was that there was no way I would win the trial. I could not believe that the entire jury was composed of *mouzhiks*, ordinary peasants, who would never be able to comprehend such a complicated case. *

If the members of the jury had been educated and scholarly, as I had expected, then I would not have been afraid of them weighing the evidence and determining my future. I did not doubt that such men would be able to understand everything involved. But *mouzhiks!* They wouldn't even be able to understand my attorneys' most rudimentary arguments. Besides, I knew how easy it would be for the officials to influence these ignorant, simplistic people who feared authority. They could

---

* The government deliberately stacked the jury with ignorant peasants believing that they were more likely to be superstitious and harbor anti-Jewish fears.

easily be bullied into believing I was their enemy, especially since I was a Jew.

The setting of the courtroom was also bound to have an effect on the jury. On one side were Russian generals and other high officials royally attired as representatives of the imperial Czar. The Prosecuting Attorney and his assistants also made a distinguished appearance, and they could be relied upon to slander me in any way possible. It is true that the jury could also see a few Russian lawyers on my side of the room, but everyone can hire advocates to defend himself. Who wouldn't be prejudiced by the contrast? The gullibility of the Russian is well-known. The wilder the rumor, the more apt he is to believe it.

The jury members were just the kind of people who would believe that the Jews used blood for Passover. For all I knew, they might already believe this idea. If that were the case, then there was nothing I could do. There was nothing anyone could do. I would have to trust in God and await the outcome. I glanced at the lawyers, both my own and those for the prosecution, Schmakov and Zamislovsky. Scanning the faces of the audience, I noticed my wife sitting in a remote corner. She sat alone, with her head down and tears in her eyes.

When I had entered the courtroom, there had been a considerable amount of activity. Many people were conversing in loud voices, others were walking back and forth. Various officials were coming in with their briefcases and reports. The confusion and din reminded me of an orchestra tuning up its instruments prior to the start of a concert.

When the Sergeant-at-arms shouted, "Silence, the Court is entering!" all in attendance rose from their benches as one. More officials came in, and immediately, it became very quiet. It even sounded as if all breathing had been suspended.

The Presiding Judge, Boldirev, broke the silence. He directed himself to me with a question.

"To what religion do you belong?" he asked.

I did not recognize my own voice as I answered in a tone approaching a shout, "I am a Jew."

I noticed that the District Attorney and the lawyer for the prosecution, Schmakov, exchanged smiles when I exclaimed that I was a Jew. Instantly, the lawyers of both sides became embroiled in an argument. The Presiding Judge asked my lawyers if they objected to the prosecution lawyers being seated so near to the jury.

Karabchevsky answered at once. "Yes, we are most emphatically against that. They are sitting too close to the jury, and every word they utter is liable to sway them."*

The prosecution attorneys denied the charge, but they were over-ruled.

Then came the administering of the oath to the witnesses. This was no trifling matter. One hundred and thirty-five witnesses were summoned for the defense and thirty-five for the prosecution, making a total of one hundred and seventy witnesses. As the witnesses were being sworn in, the silence that had prevailed gave way, and once again, the babel prevailed.

As each witness came up to take his oath, he had to pass by my seat. All of my witnesses paused a moment to greet me. Even a number of witnesses who had been called by the prosecution

---

* Secret police were disguised as court attendants and stationed next to the jury in order to eavesdrop on their private conversations.

acknowledged me with friendly smiles. This swearing-in procedure lasted the entire day and well into the night, and I was forced
to sit there the entire time, as if nailed to my seat. I almost fainted
from the boredom and exhaustion. When it was all over, I was
transported back to the prison in the black coach.

All during my imprisonment, I had slept on a floor that was
practically bare, and no one had ever considered making it any
more comfortable for me. In fact, if anything, the reverse was
true, and they tried to make me as miserable as possible. I was
thus shocked to discover that a cot with a mattress had been
placed in my cell. And the guards acted like such friends, I hardly
recognized them. I could not figure out the reason behind their
change of heart. Did they feel I would soon be liberated and the
whole bubble of lies would burst? But the trial had barely begun!

Apparently, an order had come down from the superiors that
I should be treated more civilly for the time being. I thanked God
for that. I was happy for any relief, even if it was only for one hour.
I collapsed on the cot and fell asleep.

Diverse Witnesses

The next morning, I was once again escorted to the courthouse with the same pomp and ceremony, accompanied by squads of cavalrymen and gendarmes who acted as if they were part of an honor procession. And also, just as the day before, the courtroom was packed, but this time, a nervous tension could be sensed. Yesterday had been spent formally administering the oaths, but today the real drama was expected to begin. The audience wanted a show.

The examination of witnesses began. The first called to the stand were the carters and drivers, those who had carted the bricks from the factory. The testimony from these witnesses was expected to be relevant to a crucial part of the trial.

According to the indictment, the lamplighter at the factory, Schakhovsky, had sworn to the Prosecuting Attorney that on Saturday, March 12, at nine o'clock in the morning, he had seen me standing in my house with two *tzaddikim* who were dressed in their long caftans and skullcaps, wrapped in *talleisim** and absorbed in prayer. After the prayers were finished, I was alleged to have chased Yustchinsky around the factory yard, caught him and carried him away to the kiln where the bricks were baked. Schakhovsky said he didn't know exactly what had taken place after that, but it was quite clear that Andriusha had not escaped my hands alive. Schakhovsky also testified that no one was around the factory at that time, not even the workers.

Zhenia, Tchebiriak's little boy, had told the same story to Fenenko. When the prosecutor asked me at the time what I had to say in regard to Schakhovsky's testimony, I explained to him that there was a receipt book system in operation at the factory. The receipts showed who the drivers and carters had been that day and to whom the bricks had been delivered. The carter who loaded the bricks and delivered them to the customer had to enter this information into the book and sign his name. The log thus revealed that on the twelfth of March, fifty drivers and carters had been engaged to deliver ten thousand bricks that day. It took the entire day to complete the order. It was, therefore, preposterous for anyone to assert that the factory yard was empty or that I had nothing better to do than chase after Andriusha Yustchinsky.

When one of the drivers was summoned to testify, he declared, "We were always at the factory. We even slept there. Beilis lived on the upper floor, and we lived on the lower one. We all know that Beilis is an honest man."

Another driver had more to relate on my behalf. "Beilis used

---

* Prayer shawls

to get up very early, about three in the morning. Whenever we would knock on his door, he was always ready. He was a very diligent, faithful employee, and he used to watch us closely to make sure we also got up early and went to work on time. Very often, he would have to leave his table in the middle of a meal to come and supervise us to see that we were not loafing. He never had even an hour's rest from his responsibilities. All of us Russians were always around, day and night."

The simple, modest testimony of these drivers, who were plain, unpretentious peasants, made a strong impression on the entire assemblage.

The next witness was a woman whom I had never seen before. The Presiding Judge asked if she knew me.

"Yes, sir, I do know him," she replied. "He is Beilis, and it is his fault that my life has been ruined. I lost my husband because of him. My husband was a locksmith, and one day, he needed a short piece of metal that he could not find anywhere. He noticed a similar piece of metal at Zaitzev's factory, so he took it, thinking that Zaitzev would not notice the loss of that one little piece since he was such a rich man. However, Beilis did not let the matter drop and brought charges against my husband. While in jail, my husband became infected with typhus and died. Even though he destroyed my happiness, I must admit that Beilis is an honest man who is true to his employer and carries out all his duties honorably."

One witness after another was summarily brought forward, each giving testimony that tore to shreds the charges contained in the indictment. For those who were really interested in the truth, nothing could have been clearer than the straightforward, unadorned testimony of these plain people. Unfortunately, there was no way to tell how the jury had reacted, and they were the ones who counted.

The next witness to appear before the judge was an elderly Polish man by the name of Vissimirsky. He was a neighbor who lived three houses away from me. His story was so fascinating that the audience sat spellbound throughout his entire testimony. He made such a powerful impression that a hubbub erupted when he finished.

Vissimirsky was a cattle trader. Every time I needed a cow, I bought one from him. He was also a daily visitor at my house and, as such, knew all there was to know about my family. Vissimirsky knew that at the time of the murder I did not own a cow. Since Vera Tchebiriak and her children had testified that they had come to my house on March 12 for the purpose of buying milk, his testimony to the contrary was a blow to the prosecution.

Now I understood why Fenenko had asked me whether I had a cow and sold milk. Vissimirsky stated most emphatically that all the stories about the cow and the milk were absolutely false, since he knew for a fact that I had not had a cow during that entire year.

When he completed his testimony, he still remained standing before the judge, as if absorbed in thought. It was clear that there was more he wanted to say. There was absolute silence in the courtroom; everyone was all eyes and ears, wondering what it was that this old gentile gentleman knew, what it was he wished to tell. Why was he hesitating so long?

I myself felt quite uneasy. I knew he had told the truth about the cow, but I also couldn't imagine what more he had to add.

"There is something else I'd like to say," he stammered. "I-I didn't know I'd have to be a witness. After all, what do I know about courts and trials and things? I am over sixty years old with one foot in the grave already. I've lived a full life, and I never had to come to court, either as a witness or a defendant or anything, and I expected to die without ever stepping into a courtroom. But I received the summons to come, so I'm here."

He paused, as if gathering the courage to continue and, turning to the judge, haltingly began again.

"This case has made me ill for over two and a half years. I know that it has shortened my life. I want you to know I only have one son whom I love dearly, so I wouldn't do anything dishonest or ungodly that might cause him shame. Besides that, I am under oath, and I believe in God and fear Him. So I cannot keep silent any longer. I must tell you everything I know. You have enough proof from what I've testified about the cow to know that the charges against Beilis are false. But I'm going to tell you more, something that will put an end to all these tales about Mendel Beilis being a murderer, that he murdered Andriusha Yustchinsky and used his blood for the Passover *matzos*. I am going to prove to you once and for all that all these charges are false."

A silence gripped the courtroom. All that could be heard was Mr. Vissimirsky struggling to control his emotions. When he finally spoke, it was with great difficulty.

"I come from the city of Vitebsk, where I had been the manager of an estate on the outskirts of town. I had an assistant, a dear friend and co-religionist by the name of Ravitch. We both moved to Kiev at the same time and lived near each other. It so happens that our homes were close to the Tchebiriak house. The

Ravitches were kind, gentle people who had no children. They had a grocery store that supported them quite comfortably, and they lived an honorable life. They had made a good life for themselves and were content.

"Then one day, out of the clear blue, Mr. and Mrs. Ravitch came to see me to say good-bye! They said they were leaving the country! I was amazed. I could not imagine why they had to leave so suddenly. This had been their home for so many years, and they were so respected. Why should they have to leave such a profitable business and so many good friends? What was the matter? And not only that, but they were going to the other end of the world. They were leaving everything and going to America!

"When the Ravitches saw how shocked I was, Mrs. Ravitch started to cry. I was deeply moved because I knew something was wrong. With tears in her eyes, Mrs. Ravitch tried to speak. 'We have to go to America,' she said.

"'Why?' I asked. 'Why in the world would you undergo such hardships in a foreign country? Do you have any friends or relatives there?'

"Mrs. Ravitch broke down and couldn't say a word. Mr.Ravitch also couldn't talk. It was obvious that something terrible had happened that they couldn't speak about. I begged them to tell me what was wrong.

"'I am your friend,' I said. 'You can trust me. Maybe I can help you.'

"'You are a true friend,' Mrs. Ravitch said sadly. 'And if we tell you, then it will endanger your life and ours. You must promise me that you will never say a word of this to anyone.'

"Of course, I gave her my word, because I had to know the

truth. What I am going to tell you," Mr. Vissimirsky said, staring the judge straight in the face, "is what Mrs. Ravitch said to me.

"'We were quite friendly with Vera Tchebiriak,' Mrs. Ravitch had said, speaking in a low, mournful tone. 'After all, we were neighbors. She would come to my house to borrow things, and I would go to hers. Sometimes, I would need a pot or some other type of utensil. One morning, I went to her house to borrow a chopping knife. We shared things so often that I knew where everything was located in her kitchen. When I saw that Vera was still in bed, I went on past her room to get the chopper myself.'"

Mr. Vissimirsky had paused frequently to catch his breath, as he was greatly distressed. Raising his voice and his head at the same time, he almost shouted to the jury, "Mrs. Ravitch told me that when she passed by the bathtub, she saw a dead child lying there. She said that she was so frightened, she ran out of the house!"

It took a few minutes for Mr. Vissimirsky to regain his composure. The secret that had eaten away at him for two and a half years was finally out. There was a murmur throughout the chamber that ceased the moment he resumed his tale.

"Obviously, Vera realized that Mrs. Ravitch had seen the body. Vera went to see Mrs. Ravitch and told her that since she had seen the dead child, she had to leave Russia right away. Vera came to warn her because of their friendship, and she said that if they did not leave, they would be killed.

"Mrs. Ravitch said she had started sobbing and cried to Vera, 'My friend, what are you saying? Leave the country? Where can I go? Why?'

"Vera had retorted, 'I will give you the money you need to get away, but you have to go to America. I know you would not report me, but once the investigators start putting pressure on you and the police send out their spies, it will be impossible for you to conceal the truth. They will be able to get the information out of you one way or another. You must disappear.'

"So what could Mr. and Mrs. Ravitch do? They fled to New York just a couple of days later."

A veritable storm arose in the courtroom when Mr. Vissimirsky ended his testimony. Vera Tchebiriak had been sitting there, awaiting her turn as a witness. She had looked like the picture of a lady, bedecked in fancy finery with a gay hat. Now she was gesticulating frantically with her hands. The Presiding Judge, Judge Boldirev, was apparently a close acquaintance, and he tried to calm her down. However, instead of calling her Mrs. Tchebiriak, as the official regulations for addressing a witness prescribed, he called her Vera Vladimirovna, as if she were a prominent person or a dear friend. The people who were sitting close to her began to move away, shunning her as if she suddenly filled them with fear.

I could see that the jury was quite taken with the whole spectacle. When Vera Tchebiriak realized that everyone, the jury included, was staring at her, she took off the hat and pulled a shawl over her head. She was visibly trembling and white as a sheet. The Presiding Judge, who was apparently quite shaken himself, confronted the witness.

"If you knew all of this, then why have you kept silent for such a long time?"

"I didn't think I'd ever be called as a witness," Mr. Vissimirsky somewhat ashamedly confessed. "Besides, I was testing my religion. I wanted to see whether our God is a righteous God, and if he would let an innocent man suffer. I really believed the truth would come out on its own."

It was clear the Presiding Judge did not want to prolong this witness's testimony for one moment longer. In fact, he wished he had gotten rid of him a long time ago.

The next witness was a ten-year-old boy. His account dealt yet another blow to the prosecution's case. He also further implicated Vera Tchebiriak. I must note that several times during the trial, not only was my innocence being heralded, but Vera Tchebiriak's complicity was proclaimed. More than one witness stated, with absolute certainty, that Vera Tchebiriak had committed the murder. The grim irony of the situation was that she had been summoned as a witness against me.

When the boy took his place on the stand, he glanced at me and smiled.

The Presiding Judge addressed him, "Do you know Mendel Beilis?"

"Yes, I know him."

"Did he ever chase you away from the factory?"

"No, I never had to be chased away, and besides, that wasn't his job. They had a *dvornik*, a janitor, for that. Mr. Beilis had other business to take care of."

The judge repeatedly asked that question throughout the trial, because the prosecution was trying to prove that I was in the habit of chasing Christian children out of the factory yard. Then they could say that one time I caught Andriusha Yustchinsky and killed him.

The boy continued his testimony. "Yes. We used to play

around the factory; but Yustchinsky was never there, and Beilis never chased us away." He then added the following statement. "Your honor, before you called me up to the stand, I was sitting near Vera Tchebiriak. She told me that I shouldn't forget to say that Andriusha Yustchinsky had been playing at the factory with us. She said that maybe I had forgotten since it was such a long time ago. I told her not to tell me what to say. I told her that Andriusha never played with us at the factory, that it was a lie. I told her that I was going to tell the truth."

I could see by the expression on their faces that the jury members were moved by the boy's words. Vera Tchebiriak's condition was deteriorating by the moment. Even though the Presiding Judge kept calling her Veritchka, or Vera Vladimirovna, she was almost in a faint. My witnesses made it clear beyond a shadow of a doubt that they believed she was the one who had murdered the boy.

During the first few days of the trial, a series of important witnesses appeared. Several workers were summoned to tell about the fire that had broken out at the factory. I didn't know about the fire, but I learned about it during the trial.

Apparently, some time after my arrest, there had been a fire at my house. It had been caused by arson, and the culprit was never discovered. I have no doubt that Vera's gang was involved. The anti-Semitic newspapers, however, began printing stories to the effect that it was my relatives who had set the house on fire, allegedly in order to destroy any evidence I might have left behind. The witnesses were therefore asked many specific questions about where the fire had broken out and when. This was important, because the anti-Semites were insisting that the fire had not been started until all the furniture had been removed from the house.

The employees stated that the fire had broken out at midnight, and if they had been asleep, they would all have perished in the flames. It was only due to a fortunate coincidence that they happened to be awake at this time of the night. One of the workers was drunk that Sunday night, and he was so sick that he began to scream and cause a commotion around midnight. He made such a racket that everyone woke up. All of a sudden, someone saw smoke and then fire coming from my part of the house. My family was fast asleep, and as one of the workers avouched, "If we hadn't rescued the Beilises, they all would have been burned to ashes."

Two young sisters by the name of Dyakonova were called up next. The testimony from one of the girls proved to be highly informative.

"My sister and I," she began, "used to spend the night at the Tchebiriak house all the time because we were very good friends with her children. One night, Mrs. Tchebiriak invited us over because her husband had to be on duty as an orderly at the telegraph office and she didn't want to be at home alone. Around midnight, after Vera fell asleep, I was walking around and noticed something on the floor that was large and wrapped in a bag. I was curious and wanted to see what it was, so I uncovered the bag. I saw a dead child lying there. I was frightened almost to death and ran to wake Vera. I started yelling, 'There's a dead child lying in there! And it looks like Zhenia!' But instead of answering me, Vera began to snore and pretended she didn't hear me. I was too afraid to stay in that house any longer, so I woke my sister immediately and we ran home in the middle of the night."

The Prosecuting Attorney and the other lawyers for the prosecution were making wry faces throughout the girl's testimony. They also tried to confuse her and make her look ridiculous. The Presiding Judge even intervened with a question. "Why didn't you tell anyone about this before?"

Undaunted, the girl replied, "We were afraid. Vera is quite a dangerous person, and she could have easily murdered us, too. Until this point we had to keep silent, but now we can tell the truth."

I could see that both the audience and the jury were deeply moved by the girl's story. The jury had exchanged sympathetic glances throughout the testimony.

Yet another witness, a barber, was called up to the stand. He recalled that one night, when he had been arrested and taken to the *Outchastok*, the police station, three other prisoners were brought in from Moscow. They turned out to be Vera's chief gangsters, Rudzinsky, Singayevsky and Latischeff. The barber overheard Rudzinsky call Latischeff a brainless beast who was stupid for "throwing him near the factory yard, near the Jew's house." He said he hadn't heard anything else. He also testified that he had told this story to Fenenko.

I would like to note that I learned of things during my trial about which I had previously had no idea. I had been kept in isolation for over two years, so it was with the greatest curiosity that I listened to the testimony presented in court. I was thus becoming informed of all that had taken place around me while I was locked behind bars. Only then did I begin to realize what

powerful evidence the authorities actually had against Tchebiriak. *
And yet I was the one sitting on the defendant's bench. How
ironic!

Another witness was a Mrs. Malitskaya. She was in charge
of a government dram shop, which is what the government
liquor dispensary was called. This liquor store was located on the
same premises as the house where the Tchebiriaks lived. The
Tchebiriaks lived on the second story, and the dram shop was on
the ground floor. Mrs. Malitskaya told the court that on the night
of March 12, she heard something heavy being dragged across
the Tchebiriak's floor. She listened closely and heard a child
screaming. She said she didn't know what was going on, but she
did know what she had heard.

---

* But no one had any idea just how much information the Minister of Justice
actually had. Immediately after the Revolution of February, 1917, the private
archives of the Czar were raided. Correspondence was discovered that revealed
that in June of 1911, even before Beilis was arrested, the authorities knew of
Vera Tchebiriak's complicity. These papers also show how the government
suppressed the additional information that Brazul-Brushkofsky and Krossovsky
tried to make public.

CHAPTER 23

More Surprises

The Presiding Judge apparently tired of listening to so much favorable testimony on my behalf. The evidence so far clearly indicated that Vera Tchebiriak had committed the murder in her own house. Whether it was Vissimirsky or the sisters Dyakonova or the ten-year-old boy or Mrs. Malitskaya, they all implicated Vera Tchebiriak. In order to offset the impression that had been made on the jury, the court began to assemble the witnesses for the prosecution.

A deacon was announced first. The prosecution felt that since he was like a priest, the peasants on the jury would be positively influenced. The witness began to speak quietly and at length, and I could see that his words were having the desired effect. The Presiding Judge began asking him the usual questions.

"Do you know anything about the murder?"

"I know a great deal," he replied smugly.

"Exactly what do you know?"

"I know that Andriusha Yustchinsky was a dear, almost saintly little boy. He wanted to become a priest when he grew up, so I was helping him prepare for seminary. When I once asked him why he wanted to become a priest, he confided that he liked the vestments very much. When I heard that he had been murdered, I was devastated. His mother asked me to participate in the funeral since I knew him so well. When the casket was about to be lowered into the grave, I saw pogromists handing printed circulars to the public. As soon as I read those circulars, I knew that the Jews had nothing to do with Andriusha's death. I realized that this tragic death was going to be used to cause pogroms against the Jews."

There was considerable movement and grumbling in the courtroom. The judge threatened to clear the hall if order was not maintained.

The next witness was a monk. He was also asked, "What do you know about the murder?"

"I am over sixty years old," he sniveled. "And I am more concerned with life in the world to come than with this life. So I must tell you the truth, and I tell you, my dear brothers, if the earth could give up its dead, then you would see how many Christian children have been murdered by the Jews."

It was obvious that the monk was about to embark on a diatribe against the Jews for the benefit of the prosecution. As a stir rippled through the hall, the Presiding Judge quickly stepped in with a question.

"Have you yourself ever witnessed such a murder, or have

you just heard about it?" he asked sternly.

"No, I've just heard about it," the monk stammered.

"Well, then, sit down," the judge said, somewhat exasperated.

The monk angrily sat down. I understand that the Presiding Judge was severely reprimanded by his superiors, and he was told that he would lose his post if he did not allow the prosecution to carry out its task.

It turned out that these witnesses were called back for cross-examination. The monk had felt it was his duty to come and defend the honor of the Russian justice system. And then to be insulted by the judge? One could know the truth, he asserted, without seeing it himself. When the monk was on the stand, it was Gruzenberg's turn to handle the cross-examination. Tact demanded, however, that a Russian lawyer and not a Jewish one should handle the task. Gruzenberg, therefore, wrote a note to Karabchevsky, and Karabchevsky proceeded with the questioning.

"Dear Father," Mr. Karabchevsky began, "I beg your forgiveness for asking you this question, but I must. Tell me, please, are you not yourself a Jew by birth?"

The monk was definitely disconcerted. He had not expected the question, and he did not like the idea of revealing his former Jewish status to the Russian people at large. Yet he had to give an answer.

"Yes," he muttered. "I had been a Jew for fifteen years."

"Did you ever hear in your father's house that the Jews used Christian blood for Passover?"

"No," he admitted. "I never heard about it in my father's

house, but I learned about these things when I became a Christian."

At this point, Mr. Karabchevsky turned to speak to the jury.

"Gentlemen," he pointed out, "the Father himself says that he had no knowledge of such things when he grew up at home as a Jew. He only learned about it after he converted to Christianity. We all know that there are Christians who invent wild stories about the Jews, and his new co-religionists must have told him this story to make him hate the Jews."

The cross-examination of the monk was thus concluded, and he was not interrogated any further. This witness also brought the day's session to a close. It was quite late in the evening, and everyone was tired. They all went to their respective homes, and I was sent back to jail.

The next morning, the first person called to the witness stand was a college student named Golubov who was one of the leaders of the Black Hundreds in Kiev.* He was dark-complexioned and looked like a real-life desperado. His appearance created somewhat of a sensation, because the prosecution had touted him as a star witness. He was expected to put on a wonderful performance.

The Assistant Prosecutor, Mr. Vipper, the Presiding Judge and the lawyers for the prosecution all greeted him with an overt display of friendliness and respect. As he walked to the stand, all eyes were riveted on his. For some reason, he was extremely

* It was Golubov who had first informed Tchaplinsky that there was a Jew maned Mendel who worked at a brick factory. As head of the Double-headed Eagles, he carried out much of the "dirty-work" that incriminated Beilis and buried the truth.

nervous and kept getting more and more pale. The Presiding Judge formally asked him what he knew about the case and the murder, yet he remained silent. This alone caused a great disappointment. He was then asked whether he felt well and was told to try and compose himself. A chair was quickly brought in for him, and no sooner had he sat down than he fell off in a swoon.

The "expert" professors who had come at the behest of the Black Hundreds, Kosortov and Sikorsy, were also in the courtroom at this time. They turned to the famous Professor Pavlov, who was the personal physician of the Czar and who was also there as a witness. They pleaded with him to help Golubov regain consciousness.

"Well don't just sit there," Dr. Pavlov replied. "He's your witness, so you do something."

Finally, attendants came and carried Golubov out, half dead and incapable of testifying. He had not been able to articulate one word. Was it pangs of conscience? No one knew what had happened to him, but my best guess is that he was afraid to face my galaxy of lawyers. He knew he would have been cross-examined by the greatest legal talents in Russia, and he may not have remembered all he had been told to say by the Prosecuting Attorney. Of course, had he told the truth, there was nothing to fear.

I feel compelled to say that Golubov's father was a very fine and noble person. He was a professor at the University of Kiev and possessed an impeccable reputation. When Golubov's father was once asked why he had permitted his son to be involved with such a nefarious group, he had reportedly replied,

"What do you want from my son? You know that he spent some time in the insane asylum of Vinnitza. It was after they sent him back home that he joined the Black Hundreds. It wasn't hard for them to lead him astray. They even made him a secretary of the Double-Headed Eagles. Would you believe that he is their leader? He is a poor, misled, unbalanced misfit. Just leave him alone, and don't mention his name to me again."

CHAPTER 24

Slander and Lies

After Golubov was hauled away, a priest by the name of Schaievitch was called to the witness stand. He had quite a story to tell.

"A lady who lived near my house," he recalled, "had wanted to build a big house for herself. One day, a Jewish money broker went over to her and asked her if she needed any money to finance the project. If so, he said, he would be able to procure for her any sum she might need. The lady told the Jew that she didn't need any money from him at all, but he was not so easily dismissed. 'Impossible,' he said. 'No matter how much money you have, everyone needs more when it comes to building a house. I know, because I have a lot of experience in these matters.' The lady steadfastly refused his assistance, and he was finally forced to leave. A few days later, he returned and again hounded the woman. He mentioned to her that he was appearing as a witness at the Beilis trial. This time the lady had an even more difficult time getting rid of him, so she told him she would think the matter over and he should come back the next day. Since I am her priest, she came to see me and asked for my advice. Should she take the money or not? I told her not to take any money from a Jew and to chase him out the next time he comes. I told her not to have anything to do with him whatsoever."

It was plain to see that the audience was not very taken with this priest's "revelations." He had not given any names or proof of any kind. It was a pure fabrication from beginning to end about some Christian lady and some Jew. The whole story was so clumsily concocted that it didn't even make sense. Many people in the audience were even amused and smiled broadly.

After that fiasco ended, the Court Clerk began reading aloud the deposition of a witness who was unable to appear in person. His story fared just as poorly as the previous one. Perhaps this was the reason the witness did not want to appear personally in court.

According to the deposition, this witness claimed that he had been in prison with me. I had already been there when he was put in jail. And why was he incarcerated? Apparently, he was some type of court official, a solicitor, who had something to do with cases while they were being processed in court. In connection with one of his cases, some important papers and documents had disappeared. Since he was in charge of handling those cases, both he and the Court Clerk were accused of wrongdoing and imprisoned.

Well, according to the story, he was brought into my cell, and when I heard that he was an official of the court, I embraced him and kissed him and begged him to use his connections to save me. We were alleged to have become close friends. Supposedly, I disclosed to him the sordid circumstances of Yustchinsky's murder and beseeched him to help me get out of this mess. I had detailed to him all the secrets of the "ritual" and given him the inside scoop. I had told him that in order to perform a ritual murder, one needed the participation of a physician who knew which thirteen spots on the human body could be stabbed in order to draw the most blood. I was alleged to have confided in him the name of the doctor so that he could get in touch with him when he got out. This doctor would then give him hundreds of rubles to aid him in "fixing" the case.

Who was this mysterious witness? It turned out that he actually was a prisoner who had been jailed for some crime and was in danger of being sentenced to a "military imprisonment," which was a very severe penalty. In his desperation, he thought of writing a letter to the Minister of Justice stating that he had some important evidence to give against Beilis. If his freedom could be arranged, he would be happy to tell all he knew and help them procure my conviction.

The Minister of Justice was the notorious Schtcheglovitoff who fell for the bait and believed he had found a prized witness. The Minister gave orders for the man's immediate release, and he was promptly freed by the court officials, who had no choice but to follow orders. However, when he began to give his "testimony," the judicial authorities realized what had happened, but they thought that perhaps there was a chance that the stupid peasants on the jury might believe such a preposterous tale if it were properly rehearsed. But no amount of rehearsing would have enabled this witness to survive the cross-examination by my lawyers. Therefore, he was "unable" to make a personal appearance in court.

The moment the reading of the deposition concluded, Gruzenberg jumped up and inquired why such an important witness had not been brought to the court. The Presiding Judge rejoined that the witness could not be found. The authorities had lost his address.

The next witness's testimony was also read to the jury. It was now Kozatchenko's turn, and he also declined to testify in person for fear of cross-examination. In his deposition, he stated that we had shared the same cell for several months and that, during that time, we frequently discussed Andriusha's murder. Since I had known that Kozatchenko was to be released shortly, I had allegedly asked him to do two things—to get a letter to my wife and to have some witnesses poisoned. (Adverse witnesses, of course!) The lamplighter who had testified against me and a certain shoemaker were to be included. I was alleged to have told him he would be given strychnine by a doctor at Zaitzev's hospital. I was further said to have promised him he would be handsomely rewarded by "certain Jews."

After this story was read, Gruzenberg again demanded to know why such an important witness was not ordered to appear in person. After all, my lawyer pointed out, much of the indictment was based on this man's statement. The Presiding Judge answered that the police were unable to locate this witness as well.

CHAPTER 25

The Tzaddikim

A sense of real excitement filled the air when the Sergeant-at-Arms announced that he was bringing the two "*tzaddikim*" to the witness stand. Their names were Ettinger and Landau, and they were alleged to have been seen at my house dressed in caftans and skullcaps and wrapped in *talleisim*. Shakhovsky the lamplighter had testified that on the Sabbath morning before the murder, he had seen two *tzaddikim* enter my house. The authorities checked the register at the factory office and found listed the names of these two Jews.

Mr. Ettinger was a young man about thirty years old who was clean shaven and completely assimilated. He was hardly much of a Jew at all. He was extremely wealthy and was the brother-in-law of Mr. Zaitzev. Mrs. Zaitzev was his sister.

Ettinger was an Austrian who had once come to Kiev to visit his sister's family. As a foreign Jew, he had no right to live in

Russia outside of the Pale. Even though his brother-in-law was a millionaire, an exception could not be made. Zaitzev himself lived in Lipki, the most aristocratic section of Kiev, and this was where the dashing young Mr. Ettinger had no right to reside. He could not legally be registered as a resident of that house, so he followed the usual procedure for situations such as this. He bribed a police captain in Zaitzev's district to find a way to circumvent this technicality.

The idea was to have Mr. Ettinger register as a resident of the Plossky district where Jews were allowed to live. This is what he did, although he basically continued to live in Mr. Zaitzev's house. This constituted legal compliance, Russian style. He was officially registered as a resident of the factory which was in the Plossky district, but as a matter of fact, he didn't even know where it was. He had never even stepped foot there. Why would a debonair young man, who had come to Kiev to live it up, want to go to a brick factory? To learn how to bake bricks?

Mr. Landau was in a similar predicament. He was a young man, twenty-five years old, who was studying on the continent. He was a grandson of old man Zaitzev and was also registered as a resident of the factory for the same reason. The register showed that both these men had "resided" there, but that they had "checked out" about five months before the murder had taken place. Nevertheless, the two young men were summoned as witnesses for the trial. After all, the prosecutors needed to find two Jews somewhere since the investigators had discovered that two *tzaddikim* had also participated in the murder.

When the two neatly dressed young men were put on the stand, Mr. Gruzenberg, who was well-known for his wit, introduced them to the judges and the members of the jury.

"As you can see," he said, "these gentlemen are the two *tzaddikim* who are said to have been praying wrapped in *talleisim* and dressed in caftans and skullcaps."

Since most of the residents of the city of Kiev knew a great deal about Jewish dress and customs, peals of laughter resounded through the court. They got the joke.

Mr. Ettinger could not speak Russian, so an interpreter accompanied him to the stand. Surely, he had never dreamed he would be required to answer questions of this nature. He was asked whether he was a *tzaddik* and if he ate *shmurah matzah.* * The prosecutor drilled him about eating the *afikoman* and participating in other religious rites.

He repeatedly shrugged his shoulders, but he patiently answered all the questions. The whole situation must have seemed unreal to him, as if he were in an insane asylum. As soon as he answered a question, his reply was immediately translated into Russian.

The Prosecutor, Mr. Viper, was the one who had drafted the part of the indictment that mentioned *tzaddikim*. He became quite nervous listening to the testimony, for it certainly did not coincide with his version of events. He also could not understand why a Jew would deny being a *tzaddik* and eating *shmurah matzah*.

---

* *Matzah* that is made from wheat that has been guarded since harvest by a *shomer*, "a watchman," to insure that it meets the strictest standards of Jewish law. Unfortunately, the added protection afforded this *matzah* only served to confirm suspicion that this *matzah* was indeed the product of some mysterious religious rite.

Mr. Viper angrily turned to the witness and snapped, "I also speak German, and I understood every word you said. Now why don't you tell the truth?"

He wanted to give the jury the impression that all of Mr. Ettinger's testimony had been a lie. It did not occur to the jury that the Prosecutor would publicly make such a false accusation, so they presumed he was telling the truth. Mr. Viper had succeeded in casting aspersions on Mr. Ettinger's integrity, and the jury began whispering among themselves.

How could these unsophisticated farmers be expected to comprehend that it was not possible for this handsome, well-to-do, modern young man, who spent his nights partying with chorus girls, also to be a *tzaddik* who ate *shmurah matzah*? Tears of frustration must have contorted my face, for when Viper saw my expression, he began to laugh. The more he mocked me, the more embittered I became, causing him to laugh that much louder. Unfortunately, it appeared to the jury that it was the veracity of Mr. Viper's accusation that had upset me. Nothing could have been further from the truth.

I had previously mentioned that Vera Tchebiriak had told the Prosecutor how she had been invited to the city of Kharkov to see a prominent person who would give her forty thousand rubles to take the blame for Yustchinsky's murder. She later stated that this person was Mr. Margolin, my lawyer. She also claimed that Mr. Sergei Yablonovski, an associate editor of the *Kievskaya Mysil*, was also present at this clandestine meeting.

It was now Mr. Yablonovski's turn to take the witness stand. He bluntly declared that he had never been to Kharkov. Madame Vera Tchebiriak was called upon to refute his testimony. The

Presiding Judge got straight to the point. He asked her if she would recognize the man who allegedly offered her that money in Kharkov.

"Of course, I would recognize him," she said.

Yablonovski was asked to approach the bench. The Judge proceeded with his questioning of Vera.

"Do you know this man?"

"If he sits down in a chair, then I'll recognize him," she replied.

The Judge turned to Yablonovski.

"Is what Vera Vladimirovna told us true? Did you and another man offer her money to take the blame for Andriusha's murder?"

Yablonovski smiled. "One of us is telling the truth. It is up to you to decide who is the liar."

"Well, Vera?" the Judge asked.

"I'll be happy to sit down if you'd like," Mr. Yablonovski offered with a smile. A chair was brought over, and he made a big production of sitting down and folding his hands in his lap.

"Yes, yes!" Vera exclaimed. "That's him! That's the way the man who offered me the money was sitting, with his hands folded just like that."

A roar of laughter again erupted in the courtroom. Even the Presiding Judge was bemused. "How is it that you can recognize him by the way he sits and not by his face? Don't most people recognize someone by the face?"

She smugly responded, "Well, on that occasion, he was sitting just as he is now, and that is why I recognize him."

The audience thoroughly enjoyed this interchange, and I

myself even found it hard to suppress a laugh.

It was finally time for the lamplighter, Mr. Shakhovsky, to appear. The entire assembly was waiting for the spectacle to continue. Since much of the indictment rested on his eye-witness testimony, he was considered a key witness for the prosecution.

"What can you tell us about this case?" the judge asked.

To everyone's astonishment, Mr. Shakhovsky replied, "I don't know anything about it."

The Court Clerk scurried to find Mr. Shakhovsky's deposition wherein he had described how, on that Saturday morning at nine o'clock, he had seen the *tzaddikim* with their skullcaps and *talleisim* praying in Beilis's house. All of this was read aloud in court. How could he now say that he knew nothing? Nothing!

"I'll tell you the truth," Mr. Shakhovsky mumbled sheepishly. "When I said those things, I was drunk. A detective, Mr. Polishtchuck, kept giving me vodka. Besides, I was angry at Beilis because he threatened to have me arrested for stealing wood from the factory yard. It's true. I did say all those things, but I wasn't under oath. I swear, this time I'm telling the truth. I am a Christian, and I fear God. Why should I destroy an innocent man?"

It was as if a bomb had been thrown into the courtroom. All the Black Hundreds who had come to watch were completely dumbfounded. The whole scenario for the crime had been built upon the lamplighter's story. Now what could be done? The disappointment was all the greater because so much had been expected. Schmakov and Zamislovsky leaped to their feet and began to try and salvage Mr. Shakhovsky's testimony.

"Don't you remember," Schmakov almost begged, "when

you told me about that woman named Volkovna who had met your wife and made fun of you because you lived so close to the scene of the murder and didn't know anything about it even though the whole world knew it was Beilis who had murdered Andriusha?"

"I know nothing. I was drunk."

"But didn't you say—"

"I was drunk I tell you, I don't know a thing."

Mr. Shakhovsky's wife was hustled to the stand.

"I don't know anything about any of this," was all she could say.

"But what about your conversation with Volkovna? Please tell us what you said to her."

"She was the one who did the talking," Mr. Shakhovsky's wife answered sullenly. "And it was all nonsense anyway. But if you want to know what she said, ask her."

Madame Volkovna was escorted to the stand. She turned out to be quite an old peasant woman, barefoot and clothed completely in rags.

Again, the same question. "What do you know about this case?"

Volkovna proved to be a testy character who was quite irate about being dragged to court. "Leave me alone, all of you. I don't know a thing," she protested.

"Will you tell us what your profession is?"

"What do you think I do? I collect alms whenever I can get them."

"What do you do with the money?"

"When I can, I buy some vodka to drown my sorrows."

Naturally, the audience laughed, but the prosecutor ignored it and went on.

"The Shakhovskys told us that you had been bragging that you knew all about the case and they didn't."

"Will you leave me alone?" the aged beggar almost shouted. She had become even more agitated. "What do you want from an old lush like me? I was probably drunk that day, too, and slept on the street. Now leave me alone, and stop pestering me."

Her entertaining performance had delighted the courtroom audience. Even the judge couldn't help but grin.

CHAPTER 26

More Lies Exposed

The testimony thus far presented in court seemed to indicate that the truth would emerge victorious. Not only were the witnesses for the defense proving my innocence, but even those called by the prosecution inadvertently helped my position. The case against me had been dealt a severe blow by Shakhovsky, whose performance was a terrible disappointment for the prosecution. Everything appeared to be going my way, but when I would glance at the homely features of the jury, a chill would run down my spine. I could not discern how they were responding to the testimony. I feared they were being overwhelmed by the procedural technicalities and would fail to grasp the import of the whole affair.

At the end of a short intermission, Mr. Krassovsky was summoned to the witness stand. Mr. Krassovsky had formerly been a detective with the secret police force and had risen to the rank of captain. He had retained that position for twenty years and had distinguished himself by his cleverness and efficiency. He had the reputation of being able to solve any murder or other capital crime. He had, however, been out of the limelight for many years.

When Yustchinsky's murder first came to light, the public had demanded that Krassovsky be put in charge of the police investigation. He enjoyed their full confidence and respect. The problem was that the Black Hundreds did not want Krassovsky involved; they were afraid he might actually find the real murderers, and this was the last thing the anti-Semites wanted. Six months later, when my lawyers insisted that the investigation be handled by a police official who was both competent and trustworthy, Krassovsky was put in charge. He immediately picked up the right scent and was about to indict the whole gang when the Governor himself interfered. A trumped-up charge of misconduct was levelled against Mr. Krassovsky, and he was demoted and thrown into jail. This was just the first of many humiliations he was forced to endure. A lawsuit was even filed against him. He was ultimately acquitted, but he lost his commission and was never reinstated as a police detective. This was the price he had to pay for his sin of trying to uncover the truth.

Mr. Krassovsky did not speak for very long, but what he said was quite sufficient. He described his activities as they related to Vera Tchebiriak.

"When I was investigating the murder, I visited the Tchebiriak house quite often. During the time Vera was in prison, her two children, Zhenia and the girl, both fell ill and were taken to a hospital. Immediately upon her release from jail, Vera ran to the hospital to take the children home, even though she was warned by the physicians not to do so. The boy was so weak they feared he might die on the way. But she would not listen to reason. She insisted on taking them home at once. She was afraid they might say something to betray her.

"Even when I would visit the family, she was afraid of what the children might reveal to me. When I used to see the boy at home, I would ask him questions. Once, while I was sitting and talking with him, he turned pale and stopped in the middle of a word. I quickly turned and saw his mother standing behind me, making a sign with her finger for him to keep silent. Once when I came in, Zhenia was in bed not feeling well. I overheard Vera admonish him, 'Remember, you don't know a thing.' I also heard Zhenia retort, 'Mother, are you ever going to stop giving me orders and telling me lies?' A short while later, the boy was dead."

Krassovsky and Brazul-Brushkovsky, the journalist, both revealed many new facts in the course of their testimony. This information clearly indicated that the murder had been committed by Tchebiriak and her cohorts, Singayevsky, Rudzinsky and Latischeff. No less clear and convincing was the testimony given by Mr. Margolin, who appeared in court not as my lawyer but as my witness.

During the trial, I became aware for the first time of the extent of the remarkable effort that had been exerted by Messrs. Brazul-Brashovsky and Krassovsky to uncover the identity of the true murderer. While secluded in prison, I had had no idea of how hard they had worked and what they had been able to achieve on my behalf. I had some knowledge of Mr. Margolin's involvement, but I had never imagined that real Russians* who were not Jewish, men such as Messrs. Yablonovsky, Brushovsky and Krassovsky, would actually sacrifice the security of their positions in the pursuit of truth and justice. Never in all the days of our lives, will I or my family forget these wonderful and enlightened men.

Fenenko, the District Attorney, was also summoned, and he reviewed for the court the outcome of his investigations. He concluded his testimony by saying that he could not find any grounds on which to base an accusation of murder, much less a charge of ritual murder. He maintained that he knew that the testimony of Shakhovsky the lamplighter was meaningless, but he was unable to do anything about it. Since Shakhovsky was willing to testify against me, an indictment had to be drawn up.

Mr. Zaitzev was then called upon to testify. The Presiding Judge asked Mr. Zaitzev a series of questions. Did he ever pay homage to the *tzaddikim*? Had his father ever done so? And so forth. The last question, however, was totally unexpected. Why was Beilis put in charge of baking the special *matzah* that Mr. Zaitzev had ordered for his private use when there were dozens of other Jews who worked for him?

This is the story about the *matzah*. The elder Mr. Zaitzev, who had died some time before the trial, was one of the wealthiest

---

* The Jews, even those born in Russia proper who had resided there for generations, were considered a separate, alien nationality and thus were not recognized as "real" Russians. Even after the rise of Communism, when all ethnic and religious distinctions were to be eradicated, the Jew was still officially labeled as such.

Jews in all of Russia. He owned fifteen sugar factories. One of his largest factories, located in Rigorovka, about twenty-five miles from Kiev, had an adjoining beet field. On that field, several acres were set aside to be sown with wheat, and from that wheat, several hundred pounds were usually set aside for *shmurah matzah*. That grain was kept in a separate granary, and Zaitzev alone had the key.

About a month before Passover, a rabbi would come, and under his supervision, about five hundred pounds would be milled for his *matzah*. The *matzah* would then be baked, packed in cases and distributed among various members of his family and friends. This was the old man's custom, which had been a family tradition for many years.

Mr. Zaitzev had involved me in the production of this wheat for about fifteen years. When I was arrested, the officials discovered in my house some correspondence between Mr. Zaitzev and myself wherein I was instructed to go to Rigorovka and get the *matzah* flour. This is what prompted the authorities to make all sorts of insinuations about the *shmurah matzah*. When the prosecutor asked Mr. Zaitzev why his father had always sent me to take care of the *matzahs*, he explained, "Mr. Beilis's father had been a very religious Jew, and he was always careful to eat *shmurah matzah*. My father had known old Mr. Beilis very well. We had some commercial dealings him. One time, I asked my father why he had selected Mendel Beilis for this task. He replied that since Mendel's father had been so religious he probably raised his son accordingly and, therefore, Mendel Beilis was someone who could be trusted to handle this responsibility."

The most important witness to follow was Vera Tchebiriak herself. Throughout the trial, one witness after another had pointed to her as the guilty party. No one even wanted to be seated next to her. Early in the trial, she had appealed to the Presiding Judge for protection, claiming that threats had been made against her life. Every time she would go home, she would ask for a policeman to escort her to protect her from an assassination attempt.

Before describing her testimony, I would like to add an interesting observation. Whenever witnesses who were supposed to testify for the prosecution got on the stand, they always changed their story. They invariably justified their change of heart by explaining that they were good Christians, and as such, didn't know anything about Jewish religious customs. They did not know for sure whether it was true or not that Jews used blood. How could an orthodox Christian be expected to know such things? But they all concurred that, once they began examining the evidence, it was clear that Vera Tchebiriak had committed the murder. That being the case, how could they accuse an innocent man of such a heinous crime? Therefore, a great deal was expected from Tchebiriak's own testimony. The prosecution was relying on her to supply them with the best evidence thus far.

As it turned out, she had nothing to add, only repeating a couple of old stories. When she was asked if she had personally seen any of the things she described, she replied that it was her children who had reported them to her. Since the children were now residents of a better world, transported there with the able assistance of their mother, it was impossible to verify the veracity of her statements.

Yustchinsky's mother was summoned next, and even she gave an altogether different version of events than was expected. When asked if she knew Beilis, she said, "No." When Schmakov asked if she had seen any Jews around the cave where her son's body was found, she said, "No."

When Gruzenberg asked whether she recognized the shirt that was shown her by the District Attorney and was considered to be an important piece of evidence, her answer was, "No, that shirt did not belong to Andriusha." This response produced quite a stir. I noticed that some of the men on the jury exchanged glances and shrugged their shoulders. When the Presiding Judge asked if her son had gone to visit the Jews during the month of March, her answer was again an emphatic "No!"

The testimony seemed to last forever, but at last, the long list of witnesses was finally exhausted. The court decided that now was the time for the next phase of the trial to take place. The jury was to be taken to the scene of the crime. They were to inspect three places personally: the factory where the murder supposedly took place, Vera Tchebiriak's house and my own.

CHAPTER 27

The Scene of the Crime

I began to feel somewhat more cheerful. For one thing, the witnesses had finished testifying. My trial was still a long way from being over, and I knew there were still many difficult ordeals to be endured, but I felt as though the greater part of the load had been lifted from my shoulders. I also welcomed the opportunity to see my house after two and a half years of imprisonment.

It was about three o'clock in the afternoon. Despite a heavy rain that made puddles of mud, the streets were packed with people. The members of the jury were surrounded by cavalrymen and police to prevent them from having any contact with outsiders. To avoid any demonstrations, I was driven to the factory through unfrequented side streets.

At last, we arrived at the factory and approached the house which had been my home in Kiev for so many years. Since I remained in the coach, some of the neighbors came out to see me. Through the little windows of the prison coach, I could see them pointing their fingers at me and exclaiming, "Beilis! Beilis!" Some wrung their hands and wept.

The Presiding Judge finally permitted me to go with an escort into the house. My wife and children were not there, since they had been warned to leave. A new clerk, a young Christian man, was there instead.

The mud outside was so deep that we could hardly walk. Nevertheless, all of us, the judges, the jury, the experts, the people from the press, even Golubov the student, took a complete tour of the factory grounds. Everything was examined, from the place where the children used to play to the spot where "the Jew with the black beard" was supposedly sighted. The cave where the body was found was so dark that we needed to light lanterns to find our way. The factory was inspected as well.

Standing near the kiln, Schmakov, the lawyer for the prosecution, turned to the jury and said, "Look. There is a straight road from here to the cave where Andriusha's body was found."

Mr. Karabchevsky quickly interjected, "But permit me to point out that the road from Tchebiriak's house to the cave is shorter and straighter."

We went to Tchebiriak's house next. The police had brought along a little Christian boy to re-enact the murder. They took him to Vera's rooms on the top floor, held him tightly and told him to scream. The lawyers Zamislovsky and Grigorovitch-Barsky remained downstairs and said that the screaming could be heard quite distinctly.

It had taken about two hours to stage this scene. Afterwards, I was sent back to the jail, and the others went home.

Since the beginning of the trial, the prison officials had treated me with unexpected consideration, respect and friendliness, eagerly fulfilling, instead of insolently ignoring, my every request. This time, when I returned to the jail from the outing, the officials tried to outdo each other in extending to me every courtesy. Whether my jailers were metamorphosized into sensitive human beings because of orders from their superiors, or because they realized from the testimony that I was innocent, I could not tell, nor did I care. The results were what mattered most.

The next morning in the prison coach on the way to the trial, a bomb exploded. There was a mad rush of confusion outside, and I was petrified that the attack had been directed at me and would be repeated. The coach immediately halted, but the officers ordered the driver to continue quickly and take me away. The authorities never discovered the reason for the assault or the people behind it, but I later learned that a cavalry soldier who was one of the escorts assigned to protect me had been so badly wounded by the blast that his leg had to be amputated.

This day was to be spent hearing the testimony from the various scientists and religious experts. The previous witnesses had only been asked to tell what they knew about the murder. The first part of the trial had been devoted to trying to ascertain what had actually happened. Now the emphasis was on the motive. The experts were to shed light on the hows and whys of ritual blood murders. It was for them to prove either that the Jews made a practice of using Christian blood in the baking of the

Passover *matzahs*, or that all these stories were infamous lies.

The star witness for the prosecution was the Catholic priest Pronaitis. He was not a reputable Russian Orthodox priest; indeed, one could not be found to do such "dirty work" at the bidding of the authorities. They were lucky to have found someone like Pronaitis at all. He was presumably well versed in both the Talmud and *Kabbalah*. In short, he presented himself as a great Hebraist and was introduced to the court as such. But when this "expert" began to speak, it was obvious to all that he was nothing short of an ignoramus, his only talent being the ability to talk a good game. However, since the authorities needed his long-winded verbiage to carry some weight, they feigned to respect him as a holy man of great stature.

He began his lecture by stating matter-of-factly that the Jews offered human sacrifices and the Jewish religion commanded its adherents to murder gentiles. He even "interpreted" a sentence from the Talmud that supposedly said, "Murder the best of the gentiles." In the same vein, after finishing with the Talmud, he went on to the *Kabbalah*.

However, in spite of all this, when the procurator asked him if he had any direct knowledge of Jews using Christian blood, he said he did not. His expert opinion had made an impression on no one. In fact, many in the audience occasionally laughed out loud when he clearly became confused and couldn't even intelligibly answer some of the questions asked by my lawyer.

A minor sensation was produced when the testimony dealt with the number thirteen, a number which was supposed to have great significance when used in a Jewish context. The prosecution insisted that the thirteen wounds which Professor Sikorsky had discovered on Andriusha's body proved that they had been inflicted in accordance with "Jewish ritual." When it was discovered afterwards that there were actually fourteen wounds, the ritual murder charge lost even more credibility.

Furthermore, all the perverse and ridiculous lies that Pronaitis had postulated were completely refuted by the brilliant, decisive testimony given by the well-known and universally respected Rabbi of Moscow, Rabbi Mazeh.* He delivered a long, detailed speech quoting passages from the Torah, the Talmud and many other books to conclusively reveal both the absurdity and the stupidity inherent in the testimony of such "experts" as Pronaitis. Any intelligent person could see that the priest had no knowledge whatsoever of the Talmud and could hardly even read a passage in Hebrew.

The problem was the intellectual level of the jury. They had listened attentively to all that had been said, but there is no doubt that they were unable to comprehend what they heard. Such things as *Gemara*, *Kabbalah* and rabbis were beyond the grasp of plain, simple peasants. I watched the jury intently throughout the day. It was they who were to be my judges. They would ultimately base their verdict on all the explanations and arguments contained in this testimony.

One thing bothered me. Pronaitis had alleged that the Jews

---

*It was during Rabbi Mazeh's extraordinary testimony that Beilis first became aware of how deeply involved the Jewish community, both in Russia and around the world, had been with his defense and began to realize the extent of the resources that had been mobilized on his behalf. Prominent Jewish personalities as diverse as Lord Rothschild from London and the Lubavicher Rebbe played important roles.

had secret books, and Rabbi Mazeh confirmed that this was so. Well, if it were true that there were secret books, then why shouldn't they believe that secret things were written in them? Why shouldn't they believe that what Pronaitis and other Christian priests said was true and that it was the Jewish experts who were lying? I concluded that if they came to the trial with a prior belief that Jews murdered Christians for their blood, then nothing could change their minds. This realization made me all the more aware of the depth of the centuries-old tragedy that had been perpetrated upon our people by black-hearted villains like Pronaitis.

CHAPTER 28

The Verbal Battle

A t last, the day arrived when the final bout would begin, when the fight for my liberation, for my very life, would draw to a conclusion. This was the day when once and for all the accusations against the Jewish people would be addressed. This was the day when both my lawyers and the lawyers for the prosecution would have the opportunity to make their closing arguments to the members of the jury.

The Prosecuting Attorney went first. He got straight to the point.

"I have spent about thirty years in the service of the Czar," he began. "It is now my task to prove, on the basis of the facts, that this man Mendel Beilis who is sitting before us on the defendant's bench, murdered Andriusha Yustchinsky, and I shall demonstrate it so clearly that there will be no doubt left whatsoever. The world awaits the truth, the world must know the truth, and it fell to my lot to demonstrate this truth to you the jury and to the world that is watching. You gentlemen of the jury are also facing a great task. It is your duty to deliberate carefully and weigh all the testimony you have heard. You must then decide what will be the punishment for a man who has committed so horrible a crime. I am not telling you that all the Jews are guilty and that pogroms should be instituted against them, but it is true that there is a religious sect among the Jews, the so-called *chassidim-tzaddikim*, who commit crimes that the non-Jewish world knows nothing about. It is they who are secretly murdering Christian children, and Mendel Beilis is one of them.*

"Even though the whole world has been deeply shocked by this crime, part of the world is in an uproar. And why? Because Mendel Beilis, a Jew," he emphasized, pointing his finger at me, "is sitting on the defendant's bench. You catch one Jew, and all the Jews get busy exercising their control and influence and untold millions to get him out. Do you remember the Dreyfus case in France?** The whole world was turned upside down

---

* The proceedings of the trial had received international coverage, resulting in an avalanche of criticism from many heads of state, including the President of the United States. Thus, in an effort to appear more "civilized" and less anti-Semitic, the prosecution instead focused the thrust of its attack on the *chassidim*, who, with their more distinctive dress and manners, made a more vulnerable target. All segments of the Jewish community, however, were painfully aware that an accusation against any Jew posed a danger to all. They had joined forces from the very beginning for a common defense.

** In 1894, Captain Alfred Dreyfus, a Jew, was convicted of treason. After a storm of international protest over the flagrantly anti-Semitic miscarriage of justice, Dreyfus was ultimately released from his years of harsh imprisonment and acquitted. Many social and political parallels can tragically be drawn between the Dreyfus case in France and the Beilis trial in Russia.

because one single Jew was arrested and convicted.*

"But let us Christians not forget the other person who is involved. It is Andriusha, who is lying in his grave, forlorn and forgotten. It is Andriusha, whose murder has not been avenged for over two and a half years. Yet who is playing the lead and getting all the attention? It is Mendel Beilis," he shouted, again shaking his finger at my face. "If such a case had involved a Christian, would anyone have said a word? Would the whole world have come to watch? Do not forget, gentlemen, that Andriusha was one of us, he was our own. It is our job not to forget him. We cannot forget him! We orthodox Christians who are wearing the cross must have the courage to avenge the Christian blood that was shed by this man."

By now the Prosecuting Attorney's performance had reached the point where a semblance of weeping was deemed appropriate, so he paused to dab at his eyes as if overcome with emotion. "Collecting" himself, he continued with a renewed fervor.

"Just imagine how scandalously this dastardly deed was done! In broad daylight, in this holy city, where there are so many cathedrals and monasteries with all the holy shrines of Russia, here of all places, the murderers seized a young child, a saintly child, a boy who had been preparing for the priesthood and butchered him. It was a Jew, motivated by his religious fanaticism, who seized this poor child, gagged his mouth, tied him hand and foot and inflicted forty-nine wounds upon one part of his body, and thirteen wounds upon another in order to draw out

---

* The most famous document proclaiming the existence of an international conspiracy of "blood-thirsty, money hungry" Jews, The Protocols of the Elders of Zion, was produced by the Russian secret police.

five pints of human blood. I do not understand how you can be so charitable, so soft and unmanly, so afraid to avenge the blood of this innocent child.

"Do you remember the beginning of the trial when the Presiding Judge asked Beilis to what religion he belonged? Do you remember how Beilis defiantly proclaimed, 'I am a Jew'? You know what he meant? He meant to tell the world that he was a Jew, and he is laughing at us Christians. He feels that, as a Jew, he can do as he pleases."

Throughout this tirade, the Prosecuting Attorney kept drinking water. At one point, he was so exhausted and drained, he asked for an intermission. I had sat completely transfixed. Every word was like a knife at my throat, stabbing me over and over. Surely, this was the kind of speech that would move the jury. These were the words they could understand. Mr. Maklakov, the famous lawyer, came over to me and heartily slapped me upon the shoulder.

"Don't worry, Mr. Beilis," he said. "Keep your spirits up. It isn't as terrible as it seems. He speaks well, but we'll speak much better."

Within minutes, the Prosecuting Attorney was again continuing his harangue. It seemed to me that there was no end to his oration. He was desperately attempting to prove that it was I who had committed the murder, only I and no one else. Of course, Vera Tchebiriak couldn't possibly have had anything to do with it, and only a wretched liar would even suggest that she did.

Among other things, he noted, "Even the worst of men have some good moments. On this very table lay the bloody corpse of the murdered boy. When Beilis was brought in to look at it, he wept. Why did he weep? Surely, it was because he felt a pang of remorse for murdering an innocent child. At that moment, Beilis was lamenting his guilt."

It was with this speech by the Prosecuting Attorney that the court session of the day came to a close. And it was with a heavy heart that many in the audience, myself included, filed out of the room for the night.

Bright and early the next morning, it was our turn to have a say. The lawyers, Messrs. Gruzenberg, Karabchevsky, Maklakov, Grigorovitch-Barsky and Zarudny, as well as the experts, Rabbi Mazah, Professor Troyitzky, Kokovtzeff and others, all delivered splendid discourses refuting each and every aspect of the Prosecuting Attorney's arguments. Not only was Mr. Maklakov a widely respected lawyer, but he was also a Christian, and as such, he vigorously took issue with some of the Prosecuting Attorney's most inflammatory assertions.

"I listened with special attention," he calmly retorted, "to that part of the procurator's speech wherein he bemoaned the way the Jews always create a ruckus whenever one of their own is caught. Well, gentlemen, I would like for you to tell me how you would behave if, for instance, we orthodox Christians were to find ourselves amongst the Chinese, and the Chinese were to accuse one of us of a crime similar to that ascribed to Beilis. Wouldn't we leap to his defense and try to arouse heaven and earth to come to his aid? Why should the procurator be so surprised at that? How could it be otherwise? How else can they protect themselves? By sitting quietly and keeping silent? Nor must you forget that we Christians have no fear of pogroms. The Jews, however, are in a constant state of fear. Should they do nothing to prove their innocence?

"And there's another thing I want to say. We heard the procurator reproaching Beilis for having wept at the sight of the pitiful corpse. We know why he wept. He was weeping because there had been a time when he was a man like all of us, free and unconcerned, and today he is living a nightmare. Are you surprised that he should weep? Why didn't the prosecutor instead speak about his celebrated witness Golubov, who was brought in with such ceremony, yet fainted outright and couldn't say a word? Why did he faint? Was it because he didn't want to make a fool of himself by being caught in a lie?"

It is difficult, of course, to recount fully all of the speeches. Some of Gruzenberg's words, however, deserve special mention, for they made a particular impression on all who heard them.

"Not long ago," he said, "I studied together with Christians. I lived with them, ate with them, enjoyed and suffered life together with my Christian friends. And now, all of a sudden, my co-religionists and I are faced with this shameful, disgraceful accusation. I am telling you now, once and for all, and you know my words will be heard by all my co-religionists, that if I found out our Torah or other religious literature taught us or even allowed us to use Christian blood, I would not remain a Jew for one moment. I am certain that Mendel Beilis must not be convicted and will not be convicted. But should he be convicted through some terrible miscarriage of justice, then so be it. Why should he be spared the misfortune that has befallen so many of our innocent brethren who have in the past lost their lives as a consequence of these indescribably evil falsehoods and lies?

Mendel Beilis, if ever you are convicted, proclaim, 'Hear, O Israel, God is our Lord, God is One.'* Be of stout heart and good cheer."

The audience was mesmerized by the power of his message. There could be no doubt of the strong impact this speech had upon the jury. They had listened to his every word. Indeed, they had paid close attention to the statements given by all my lawyers. It seemed as if the efforts by the prosecution were doomed to a disgraceful defeat. But who could foretell the thoughts within a juror's mind?**

---

* It was the Lubavicher Rebbe who had personally directed that Beilis should be advised to keep these words in his heart and on his lips.
** Even though the prosecution was aware of the weakness of the case, they felt that the jurors would find Beilis guilty on the basis of "racial hostility" alone.

CHAPTER 29

A Narrow Escape

The great day came at last. It was the 28th of October, 1913, the thirty-fourth day of my trial, and the day the jury was to render its verdict. It was also the day when I almost lost my life.

At eight o'clock in the morning, I was called, as I usually was, to the prison office. It was from there that I proceeded to the Court House. Each time, my escorts would search me and immediately depart for the courthouse. The moment the prisoner was handed over to his escort, no one else had any authority over him. Since the escort signed a receipt acknowledging that the prisoner was in his possession, the escort alone was responsible for him, and no one else could touch him.

On this particular morning, after I was already in the custody of the escort, the Deputy Warden sent word that I should be brought back for another search. The searches were emotionally and physically humiliating and amounted to an inquisition of my body and soul. In accordance with the law, my escort refused to obey the order to hand me over. However, the warden insisted, stating that a special telegram had come from the Imperial Court, from the Czar himself, ordering that I be searched with extra stringency. Naturally, my chaperone felt compelled to comply.

Though the warden could easily have asked my escort to conduct the search, he chose to use his own men, the prison guards, to carry out his wishes. I was told to undress, which I promptly did. Whenever I was searched, I had always been allowed to leave on my undershirt. This time, the official ordered me to remove my undershirt as well. I became annoyed and ripped off the shirt, throwing it in his face. He grabbed his pistol and was preparing his aim. He was so infuriated that he looked like an enraged beast.

Fortunately, my escort heard the noise and came running in. If he had not been responsible for my safety, he never would have dared intervene; but since he had already signed for me, he was afraid not to get involved. He snatched the revolver out of the Deputy Warden's hand and sounded the alarm. There was an instantaneous deluge of officials. The Chief Warden came in. He was very agitated.

"What are you doing?" he said to me. "Isn't this the last day of your trial? Why are you starting up new trouble?"

"What do you want from me?" I cried out. "Why does this man have to subject me to new insults? I've already been searched once. Why do I have to be searched again and in such an abusive manner?"

The Deputy Warden left. A few minutes later, he returned

with some papers that he ordered my escorts to sign as witnesses. He intended to press charges against me.

"Don't think you'll get away free, Beilis," he growled. "I'll square my account with you yet. You'll never escape from our grasp. You will see. We will again put you in chains."

"That is something you'll never live to see," I said.

"Oh yes, I will," he yelled back. "Even if you're acquitted, I'll see that you get a month in prison for this!"

That was, so to speak, my breakfast, a breakfast after which I might not have survived for another meal. The Deputy Warden would have been entirely within the law had he shot me. My action constituted an "assault," and he was fully within his rights to shoot. I ended up, however, with a scare and nothing more.

CHAPTER 30

A Verdict at Last

The activity in the courtroom resembled a holiday fair. It was all over; nothing remained but the finale. With proper solemnity, the Presiding Judge turned to me and asked, "Mendel Beilis, what do you have to say in your defense?"

I rose weakly to my feet. "Gentlemen, I can only say that I am innocent. I am too weary for anything else. The prison and the trial have left me bereft of speech. I only ask that you scrutinize all the evidence that you have been listening to for thirty-four days. Examine it carefully, and deliver your verdict, so that I can go home to my wife and children who have been waiting for me these two and a half years."

The Presiding Judge then delivered his charge to the jury. "Gentlemen, it is my duty to say nothing, either good or bad. I must remain impartial. But this trial has been an exceptional one. It has touched upon a matter which concerns the existence of the whole Russian people. There are people who drink our blood. There are many things that have happened here that you must not take into consideration, neither the witnesses who wanted to whitewash Beilis, nor the experts who stated that the Jews do not use Christian blood. And you certainly must not take into the account any of the stories about Vera Tchebiriak's guilt. You must disregard all this testimony and remember just one thing: a Christian child has been murdered. It is Mendel Beilis who is accused of this crime, and it is Mendel Beilis who stands before you on the defendant's bench. It is Mendel Beilis you must try!"

The judge said this and much more in his "impartial" tone. His summation astounded not only me but a great many people in the courtroom as well.* Everyone was amazed to hear the Presiding Judge speak as though he were the Prosecuting Attorney. He continued his summary sermon until sunset.

It was about five o'clock in the afternoon when the questions were finally delivered to the jury. First, they had to decide where the child had been murdered. Then they had to determine who was the murderer. At last, I was living in actuality the moment I had already lived through in my mind a thousand times. This was the moment when the peasants who comprised the jury, in whose hands my fate rested, rose from the jury box and retired to resolve these questions. I was led to my room.

It is not possible to describe the anxiety I experienced in knowing that in a few minutes my years of waiting would come to an end. In a matter of minutes, my fate would be decided. Was

---

* Even scholarly accounts of the trial proceedings remark on the outrageousness of the judge's summation to the jury.

I to be doomed to an eternal agony and my wife and children sentenced to a life of shame and grief? Or would I be reborn a new man, unfettered and free, with a full life before me?

I was again brought into the courtroom. It was time to read aloud the signed and sealed verdict of the jury. A deadly silence filled the chamber. People almost stopped breathing.

The Prosecuting Attorney, the lawyers for the prosecution and all the Black Hundreds looked about them triumphantly. They seemed assured of victory. Only two of my lawyers, Zarudny and Grigorovitch-Barsky, remained. Gruzenberg, Maklakov and Karabchevsky had left. They were afraid of an adverse verdict and didn't feel strong enough to withstand the shock.*

The jury had not yet entered the courtroom, so all eyes were directed toward the door, the door through which the "Great Secret" would soon emerge. At last, the door swung open, and the members of the jury slowly filed in.

During the thirty-four days of the trial, I had never removed my eyes from the faces of these men in whose hands lay not only my fate but the fate of all the Jews of Russia. I had wanted to gaze into their very souls. What were they thinking about, these plain Russian peasants? They had been listening for more than a month to various stories about the murder itself, about Jewish life and about our religious laws and customs. Had they believed all they were told? Did they realize that all these charges levelled against the Jews were lies and falsehoods? Did they realize that only moments earlier they had fashioned a decision that would

---

* It must be remembered that these are Beilis' words. Although he surmised that this was the reason for their absences, there certainly may have been other reasons he was unaware of.

affect the lives of millions of Jews? My life as well depended upon what they had decided. Maybe it had even depended on just a couple of jurors; maybe on just one! Dear God, can I stand it one second more?

Why is it dragging on so long? Why don't they just read the verdict? I looked into the eyes of the jurymen, searching for a clue, a glimmer of hope. I had examined them so often during the trial, but I had never seen them like this. In the past, they had always managed a friendly smile. But now, their faces were downcast and somber. They seemed devoid of emotion. It dawned on me like a thunderbolt. Guilty! They must have decided I was guilty. I tried to pull myself together and pray to God to sustain me. Let them shoot me, let them hang me, let them do as they pleased with me. I tried to find consolation in the thought that the whole world, the world of honest men, would say I had been the victim of a flagrant miscarriage of justice. All the world would know the verdict was a colossal blunder. This gave me the courage I needed to hold out till the end.

By this time, the silence in the courtroom had become funereal. I cannot describe the rigidity with which the audience held itself, afraid to stir, lest it miss a single word. The air became so intense that we felt as if we would suffocate.

The foreman of the jury rose to his feet and began reading the decision from the piece of paper he held in his hand.

"Where had the crime been committed?" he asked aloud. "The jury has decided that it was in Zaitzev's brick kiln."*

---

*Since this part of the verdict seemed to indicate that the jury accepted the prosecution's version of how the murder took place, the government contended that the jury's decision proved that the blood libel charge itself was true.

The jury had decided that the boy had been murdered in the factory where I was superintendent. Certainly then, they had decided that it was I who had committed the murder. I held my breath and clenched my teeth. If the boy had been murdered in my factory, and I was the only Jew there, then the jury would surely decide that I was in fact the perpetrator of the deed.

The foreman continued reading. "If it has been proved that the murder was actually committed at Zaitzev's factory, who committed it? Was it the defendant Mendel Beilis? Was Beilis the one who took the Yustchinsky boy and inflicted forty-nine wounds upon his body, drew the blood out of the child's veins and used it according to the Jewish religious laws? In short, is Mendel Beilis guilty or not?

"The jury has unanimously decided. Mendel Beilis is not guilty."*

I cannot adequately describe the pandemonium that broke loose in the courtroom. There were audible gasps of relief, followed by tears of elation. I myself wept like a child. My lawyer Mr. Zarudny came running and was the first to reach me. He grabbed me, shouting, "Beilis, my dear man, you are free!"

The colonel in charge of the escort guards who was standing near me, poured a glass of water and handed it to me. Mr. Zarudny snatched the glass out of his hand and didn't let me drink it. The colonel was deeply offended.

"Why won't you let me give him a drink?" he asked. "After all, he's under my care. I'm here to protect him."

---

* Even though Beilis was obviously innocent from a legal point of view, considering the political climate in Russia, it took a tremendous amount of courage for these peasants to find a Jew not guilty.

208

"No," Mr. Zarudny screamed. I had never seen him so excited. "He is not in your hands any more. Now you have no authority over him whatsoever!" He gave me a hug and kissed me. Grigorovitch-Barsky also came over.

"Let's all go," Mr. Zarudny said. "We have some wonderful news to tell our friends. There are some people we need to congratulate."

At this moment, the Presiding Judge rose again and read the official decree, which said that by order of His Imperial Majesty, I was freed and could take my place among the people in the courtroom. As a rule, this was sufficient, and after the announcement of the verdict, the guards ordinarily sheath their swords, and the defendant leaves the dock. I, however, remained seated. I did not know what to do, and the soldiers who surrounded me were still standing with their naked swords. They made no move to put them back into their scabbards.

I glanced over at the prosecution's bench and saw Schmakov. He stood as if dumfounded and was muttering to himself. When one of his friends approached him, I heard Schmakov say, "It cannot be helped. All is lost. This is a terrible blow for Russia."

There could be no doubt that the public was rejoicing over the verdict. People were shaking hands, kissing each other, shouting their congratulations to me and wiping their eyes. All these people, most of whom were very influential Russians, I had never known before the trial. I saw that many of them wanted to come over to congratulate me personally, but the gendarmes and police did not permit them to pass. So the public greeted me from a distance, with the women waving their handkerchiefs. The Presiding Judge finally ordered the room cleared.

The Russian soldiers were experts at that sort of thing, and the room was cleared in a matter of minutes. In the meantime, I was a free man and finally recognized by all as innocent Mendel Beilis. I was still sitting on the defendant's bench, surrounded by soldiers with swords in hand.

While the people were leaving the hall, an exceedingly distinguished and inordinately large Russian came over to me.

"I am a merchant from Moscow," he said with great emotion. "I left three factories, left them almost without supervision, to come spend more that a month's time here. I have been awaiting the moment of your liberation. I could not leave as long as your fate was undecided. I knew I could not rest at home. And now, the Lord be blessed, I can go home rejoicing. I am very happy to be able to shake hands with you. Mendel Beilis, I wish you all the happiness in the world."

This Russian giant was whimpering like a child, energetically wiping his eyes and blowing his nose. "God bless you, Beilis," were his last words as he was being propelled through the door.

CHAPTER 31

My Prison Transformed

I very impatiently remained sitting on the bench. My faithful guards, the soldiers, were still there. Why was I not being told to go home? Two and a half years of prison should have been enough, yet they apparently did not feel like letting go of me.

I was simply overwhelmed that the merciful Almighty who watches over the children of Israel had extended his kindness to me as well and shielded us once again from a terrible disaster. I thought of the joy that must be reigning in my home as my family and friends were being told the good tidings.*

Finally, an official informed me that the Presiding Judge wished to see me in his chambers. I felt certain that I was going to be sent home at last.

---

* Apparently, for security reasons, his family had not been permitted to attend.

In the Presiding Judge's chambers, I found the jury, those simple peasants who had tried me. When I came in, one of the jurymen tugged at my coat and smiled. I later discovered he was one of those who had spoken on my behalf. He must have been too afraid to speak up, but I almost heard the twinkle in his eyes say, "Well, we pulled you out of that one, didn't we?"

The Presiding Judge asked the members of the jury to leave, and we remained alone.

"Mr. Beilis," he said, "you are a free man. I have no right to detain you one moment further. You can go home."

I was about to bid him good night when he raised his finger, as if to say, "One moment, please."

He spoke slowly. "If you could wait, there is something I would like to discuss with you. I think it would be better for you to return to prison for the night."

I could hardly believe my ears. Had everyone gone mad? Had I endured these years of endless suffering and humiliation and at last reached the long-awaited day of my release only to be told that I should go back to prison? Why in the world should I want to do that? Why should they begrudge me the joy of finally being reunited with my family?

Of course, I should have known not to have expected anything favorable from this judge, especially after having heard his "impartial" summation. Never have I heard such an inflammatory speech.

He noticed my anxiety and apparently understood why I was so apprehensive. He tried to reassure me.

"Calm yourself, Mr. Beilis. I only suggest this to you for your own good. This verdict was one that the masses did not expect.

The fury of the mob has been aroused, and you know how difficult it is to maintain control in such a situation. Need I remind you that it was in this city of Kiev that Prime Minister Stolypin was assassinated in His Majesty's very presence? You know what that means. It did not occur so long ago. When the people are provoked, no one can be responsible for your safety. Besides, since you have been miraculously saved and have withstood the tribulations of two and a half years of imprisonment, surely you will be able to endure one more night. Do spend this night in prison, and allow the tempers to cool down. In the morning, you will be able to go home."

I sensed that he was not telling me this out of the goodness of his heart, but what could I do? I was afraid that if I refused to take his "advice," he could always find a way to do to me whatever he chose. Either way, I had no guarantees. I recalled the incident that had occurred only that morning, and I was afraid to confront the Deputy Warden again. He had threatened to kill me if he ever saw me again. Perhaps he was the reason I was being returned to jail? Nevertheless, I agreed to do as the Presiding Judge recommended.

"In that case," he said, "we must submit a formal application. What shall we give as the reason?" He thought for a minute and said, "I have an idea. Here, write in your own name that you are requesting permission to spend tonight in prison in order to return the government's clothes and to settle your account with the administration." He wrote the application, and I signed it.

Meanwhile, the Chief of Police entered the judge's chamber.

"Mr. Beilis, are you ready to go home?" he said. "I congratulate you upon your acquittal."

213

The judge shot him an irate look. He was visibly displeased with the friendly tone the Chief of Police had used to address me.

"Mr. Beilis will spend this night in prison," he said curtly. "Please see to it that he gets an escort."

I left the courthouse, and a police escort drove me back to the prison, not as a prisoner but as a free man. I was in the same black coach, but everything else was quite different. Usually, it was dark inside. This time, there was a lamp burning in one corner. Ordinarily, I had been alone. This time, the Chief of Police rode with me. He was friendly and polite and even honored me with a cigarette. We chatted the whole way to prison. He kept asking me questions and wanted to know all about my years in prison.

"Well, praise the Lord," he said. "I am so happy this business is over. The anxiety has made me ill, because I was responsible for your safe passage the entire time. It was also my job to maintain peace and quiet in this city for the two months of your trial. I had to be on constant guard to protect you from harm. I can tell you that it is no simple matter to control an angry mob. I feel a great deal of satisfaction knowing that you have been released."

Once more, we had arrived at the dark and foreboding prison building, but I felt light at heart. I was free. On one of the streets, the coach had suddenly stopped. Upon inquiring why, the Chief of Police was informed by the escort that it was because of the military patrols that had been stationed along the road in order to clear the people off the streets.

CHAPTER 32

Home at Last

The coach stopped at the prison gate. A door opened, and an entourage of prison officials and guards came out. In the past, these same people jeered and treated me in a rough, surly manner. Everyone had felt it his duty to make a significant contribution to my suffering.

"Move on," ordered one.

"Don't crawl," barked another.

"Walk like a man, you blood-drinker," yet another would say.

This time the transformation was immediately noticeable. Yesterday, I had been a villain. Today, however, I was a free man, worthy of being treated respectfully as a paragon of virtue. Not only did the officials refrain from shoving me through their gauntlet, they actually behaved like true gentlemen, even addressing me with a title completely unheard of in those halls: "Mr. Beilis, sir." The politeness increased in proportion to the distance I advanced into the prison.

A guard rushed forward with a chair. "Sit down, Mr. Beilis," he said. "You must be tired."

The warden then came over to me. This man was a cold, ruthless bureaucrat who never missed an opportunity to inflict pain. I was always referred to as the "murderer" and "bloodsucker." He often "consoled" me with the thought that I shouldn't have to wait too much longer for my appointment with the gallows. Today, however, I had a difficult time recognizing him.

"Mr. Beilis," he said, with an effusive, sickly smile. "I would like to congratulate you most heartily and extend to you my best wishes. Please allow my wife and children to meet with you."

With that, not only did he shake my hand, he also brought in his wife and son who greeted me with genuine cordiality. The whole office staff had gathered around and were vying with each other to express their warmest best wishes. Everyone seemed to be so pleased. The prison official who had threatened me with instant death that very morning, now appeared more frightened than anything else. He had no authority over me whatsoever, and he knew it.

"By the way, Mr. Beilis, did you know that we have some of your money?" the warden mentioned casually. "There are about nine rubles and fifty kopeks in your account that we'll get for you at once. We also have some of your personal belongings in the storehouse. You'll receive them later."

I was given the money and a few personal possessions. The warden read the application that I had signed in the judge's chambers asking for permission to spend the night in prison.

"No, no, that won't do," he said, shaking his head back and forth. "Guards, take this man home. He has spent enough time in prison. Let him go home and see his family." When I heard this, I forgot all about the Presiding Judge's lecture justifying the need for precautionary measures. For some reason, the danger of an out-of-control mob now seemed remote.

"Yes, I want to go home," I said softly.

Apparently, pressure had been applied on the judge from some higher authority to persuade me to return to prison. However, since the application stated that "I, myself" had sought permission to remain in prison, the warden had the right to refuse my request. He gave orders for a cab to be summoned, and a policeman was brought in to accompany me home.

It was the law in Kiev that any Jew released from prison, who did not possess the right to live in Kiev, had to first report to the police station so that he could be adequately supervised while passing through the district. I, however, enjoyed the great privilege of possessing the right to reside in Kiev because my son was a student at the gymnasium there. This was a special exception that only pertained to the city of Kiev. In all of the other cities in Russia outside of the Pale, children acquired the right of residence on account of their parents. In Kiev, however, it was the parents who acquired this sacred right of residence based on the location of the child's school. The rationale behind this ruling was that children should not be left without parental care.

Since Zaitzev's factory was situated in two police districts, Plossky and Lukianovsky, I had to go to both of their police stations. I was driven along in an impressive procession. A contingent of calvary troops rode ahead of the cab to clear the way, with two gendarmes poised on the driver's seat. When we reached the Lukianovsky police station, I was greeted by the captain of the station, who was a notorious Black Hundred anti-Semite. He let it be known that he could not stomach the sight of a Jew. He was the one who had barged into my house on the unforgettable night of my arrest.

Much to my surprise, he also suffered from a remarkable change of heart. All the authorities, including the captain, were friendly and helpful. No sooner had I entered the police station than the captain welcomed me with outstretched arms.

"I am so very happy to see you," he exclaimed, vigorously shaking my hand. "May I please ask a favor of you Mr. Beilis? I do hope you won't refuse me."

I was afraid to ask, but the words came out. "What can I do for you?"

"My daughter would like to see you. She wants to congratulate you. Will you permit her that pleasure? She is a gymnasium student who was terribly disturbed throughout your trial. Every time she read the papers and saw that events had taken an unfavorable turn, she wept like a child. She even neglected her studies because of you. She used to go around moaning, 'Oh, my God, how the poor man must be suffering.' Please, you must allow her to come and meet you."

During the delivery of this oration, the other policemen in the station stared at their captain as though he had totally lost his senses. It was a singular sight for them to witness their savage captain humbling himself, begging a Jew for a favor. It was usually the other way around. The captain obviously considered it an honor for his daughter to converse with me.

Of course, I was only too glad to accede to his request and said that I myself would be pleased to meet his daughter. The captain dashed to the phone.

"Marcia, is that you?" he said hastily. "Your friend Mr. Beilis is here, and he will see you. Come quickly."

While waiting for his daughter, he tried to ingratiate himself. "Would you like something to drink? Tea or beer? I'll prepare the necessary papers while you're waiting."

Tea was brought in. The policeman who offered me the cup, saluted me.

Within a few minutes, the captain's daughter arrived, joined by a girlfriend. The two seemed quite bashful, hesitating to come over.

"Come on, don't be shy," urged the captain. "Come say hello to your friend Mr. Beilis."

The girl finally came over and asked very timidly, "Are you really Mr. Beilis? You must forgive me for being so bold. My friend and I both used to cry for you and pray for your salvation."

The two girls seemed to have been sincerely overjoyed at the news of my liberation. I did not expect to see such honest and genuine sympathy.

"We grieved so much because of you," the girl continued. "There were whole nights when we could not sleep and instead spoke of what you must have been going through. Of course, what we imagined was probably nothing compared to reality. But now, justice and truth have prevailed. I wish you and your family all the peace and happiness in the world."

I recall this episode because this was my first encounter after my release with pure, innocent children who were the targets of all the false propaganda about the Jewish people. It was their minds that the anti-Semites hoped to poison. At that moment, I remembered the words spoken by my gentile friend Zakhartchenko, who had said, "The stones of the bridges will crumple. The truth must and will prevail."

When all the formalities were over, the captain accompanied me to the street and helped me to my seat in the cab. We now had to go to the Plossky police station. A large crowd composed of thousands of Jews who had learned that I was on the way had assembled there. The streets were packed, and the police had a difficult time keeping order. No sooner had we reached the station than a police lieutenant ran out and embraced me. He took me by the hand and led me inside. The papers had been prepared in advance, and the whole proceeding did not take more than three minutes.

The lieutenant smiled at me and offered to take me home. "I must have the honor of bringing you safely to your wife and children and seeing that your house is properly guarded. Come, let's go!"

I recognized the old neighborhood in which I had lived for so many years, but I could not have identified my own house. The one I would have remembered burned down during my imprisonment.

The minute I walked through the door, it seemed as if it had been only yesterday that I was so unexpectedly wrenched away. My heart raced with excitement and joy.

Once inside, the children fell all over me, shouting, "Father, father!" That was all they could say. They clung to me as if to insure that I wouldn't be stolen again from the protection of their arms. Together with my wife, they cried and danced.

On the day that the verdict was expected, emotions in and around Kiev ran high. They were especially volatile in my district. The Jews were understandably afraid that a conviction would unleash a terrible massacre The threat of an imminent pogrom was real. In Kiev, the Black Hundreds and other pogromist groups were poised to strike, ready to avenge themselves against the Jews as soon as possible. For them, a guilty verdict was a foregone conclusion.

The danger of an incident occurring was greatest at the factory, for this area had served as the hub for those who had been coordinating activities against me. As a precaution, my wife had decided to send three of the children away to another part of the city, and therefore, three of my children were not able to join the reunion.

Some of the neighbors began to gather. The crowds had been kept away from the yard, so there were only a few people around, most of whom were the usual residents of the factory. There were, however, many guards stationed around my house and at the gate, and they would not let anyone enter without my permission. The lieutenant who had accompanied me home took charge and sat in one of the front rooms with two other policemen. Every half hour or so, the telephone would ring from the governor's palace for an update on the situation.*

After a while, the telegrams began to flood in from all parts of Russia. There were greetings from a group of intellectuals in Czarskoye Selo, from the Jewish deputies of the Duma, from the

---

* The installation of a telephone in his home indicates the prominence he had achieved.

famous Russian writer Korolenko, from the student bodies of the Universities of Moscow and St. Petersburg and from a number of private persons, Jew and gentile alike. I tried to go to bed about two that morning. I was completely exhausted by the events of the day, not to mention the anxiety and tension of listening to the Presiding Judge's speech, of waiting for the verdict. Everything had taken its toll. I gave the lieutenant three rubles as a tip for the police messengers who were bringing the telegrams and then lay down; but I couldn't fall asleep.

The excitement of the day had been so great that sleep would not come. This was my first night of freedom. Who could sleep on such a night? Who could waste such precious free moments for sleep? I got up, had some tea and continued my conversations.

No sooner did the dawn of the next day break than virtually thousands of people began to amass in and around the house. The streetcar, which ordinarily stopped two blocks from our house, now came all the way to our front door. Somebody had rigged a big sign up in front of my house that read, "Beilis Station." It was to this stop that the street car came bringing what seemed like thousands more.

CHAPTER 33

A Rejoicing World

I had genuinely believed that once I regained my freedom, I would be able to go home and have my life return to normal, that I would be able to go back to work and live a quiet, private life with my wife and children. Yet again, however, it was circumstances and not my wishes that were to govern my daily existence. I was not allowed to be the man I once was. I had become Mendel Beilis the celebrity.

Daily, my house was besieged by people who came to see me and express their jubilation at the outcome of my trial. Not only did individuals come by, but at times, entire groups of fifty and sixty people stopped in, as if on a sightseeing tour. Cab drivers would wait at the railroad station, and upon seeing groups of Jews descending from the platform, they would run to them and ask, "Are you going to see Beilis?" A new business had developed—driving people to my house!

Dozens of automobiles always stood in front of my house. No sooner would one party leave than another would come. People brought me small gifts, mostly flowers and chocolates. It seemed that everyone wanted to bestow upon me some token of his warm regards. It wasn't long before the house resembled a candy shop in a flower garden.

I was truly touched by this outpouring of compassion. It boosted my morale tremendously and gave me a great sense of personal satisfaction. I saw that the entire world had taken an immense interest in my ordeals and had empathized with my plight. They wanted me to know that they now rejoiced with me as well. I was, of course, most grateful for their kind expressions of sympathy and good will. My hands, however, suffered greatly from the continuous handshaking and became swollen and sore.

One day, two gentlemen came to visit me. One was from St. Petersburg, the other a doctor from Lodz. Neither of them spoke, and after a few moments, the gentleman from St. Petersburg began to sob, as if he couldn't contain his emotions any longer.

The doctor chastised him, saying, "Don't cry. It might upset Mr. Beilis."

Yet just a few minutes later, the doctor had to excuse himself and walk over to the window where his own handkerchief was kept quite busy.

It didn't take long for scenes such as this, repeated day in and day out, to affect my health. I desperately needed to recuperate, both physically and mentally, from the ordeals that I had suffered over the past years. I needed a good rest, but the constant flood of visitors made that impossible. I finally went to Zaitzev's hospital.

The problem was that many of the visitors who came to my house and did not find me there became hysterical with disappointment. Some even insisted that if they could not see me, they would commit suicide. Some people had become obsessed with the need to see me in person and refused to leave without achieving their goal. They had despaired with me and couldn't relieve their distress until they saw with their own eyes that I was safe.

So I went back home, and the daily pilgrimages resumed. The police captain in charge of the guards stationed around my house used to jest that after another month of such duty he would be able to retire with all the money he had received as tips from visitors who wanted to be allowed in.

One day, a Russian priest came to see me. He entered the house and, without saying a word, fell on his knees and made the sign of the cross.

Weeping like a child, he cried, "Mr. Beilis, you know that I have endangered myself by coming here. I should not have come to meet you at all. I could have sent my good wishes in a letter, but I decided to come in person. My conscience would not let me do otherwise. I have come to ask your forgiveness in the name of my people."

He kissed my hand, and before I even had the chance to overcome my shock and respond, he quickly ran out. This incident affected me profoundly. I could not have envisioned a high Russian clergyman ever kneeling before a Jew and kissing his hand.

What strange creatures these Russian people are! On the one hand, there are the Zamislovskys, the Schmakovs and the despicable bands of Black Hundreds, and on the other hand, one can find a Russian priest coming to beg forgiveness from a Jew for the persecutions to which he has been subjected.

On another occasion, a military colonel accompanied by a college student came to my house. The colonel was a massive man with a fierce and forbidding military appearance. He greeted me and introduced the student as his son. He began pacing the room in silence, with his spurs clicking. The entire house shook with every step he took. I was overawed. At last, he stopped and turned to me.

"Permit me to congratulate you on the outcome of your trial. I am stationed with my regiment and my family in the Far East, but I took a special leave for a month in order to come here. I had to see you in person."

This just further illustrates how difficult it is to judge the soul of a Russian. Who would have believed that this huge, gruff military officer who carried himself with the air of an executioner was capable of such a kind, noble gesture?

We exchanged a little idle talk, but for the most part, he was silent. Conversation was not his forte. It seemed as if there was something he wanted to say yet was incapable of saying. Finally, he arose, bid me farewell and left with his son.

A moment later, the bell rang. It was the colonel once more.

"You must forgive me, Mr. Beilis," he said. "Please allow me to spend a few more minutes with you. I am going to be returning to very distant lands, and I know we probably won't ever see each other again."

Before he left, he asked for one of my cigarettes. I was sorry to see him go.

The famous Russian writer and friend of the Jews, Vladimir Korolendo, also came to my home.

"You know," he confided, "I have been envious of you. I would have gladly donned your prisoner's uniform and sat in jail for you. You must have suffered greatly, but you suffered defending the truth."

Among the letters I received was one from a lady in St. Petersburg. "I am a Christian, from an illustrious military family," she wrote, "but the militaristic mentality has not affected me. Jews have always been dear to me, and I know it is a treacherous lie to say that your people want our blood. The truth is that we want your blood. It gives me great joy to know that you are free. My child also shares my feelings. During your trial, he used to look at your picture and exclaim, 'That poor man. How much he must unjustly suffer, all on account of that murderess Vera Tchebiriak.'"

During this time, the rumor began to circulate that I was receiving substantial sums of money. The truth is that some ordinary people did, on occasion, send me a few rubles, although I don't know why they did. But the papers reported that I was becoming a millionaire. The result was that I was deluged by hundreds of requests for financial aid. Talmud Torahs, rabbis, hospitals, charitable institutions and innumerable committees all beseeched me for money. Students sought funds for tuition, and people even asked for dowries to help marry off their daughters. Other people expected me to rescue them from some dire financial predicament. And these requests were for considerable sums, often thousands of rubles. I don't recall anyone asking for less than a few hundred.

The truth is, I needed help for myself. All my savings had been exhausted, and I had no idea what the future held in store for me. To live the life of an ordinary worker, as I had lived before, seemed out of the question.

Among the numerous letters of sympathy that I received, were also a number of death threats from anti-Semites like the Black Hundreds. I could not feel secure about anything, not even my personal safety.

CHAPTER 34

Provisions for the Future

T he death threats continued. As each day ceaselessly brought its ever increasing quota of ominous notes, the Governor of Kiev insisted that I leave the city, claiming that he could not be responsible for my safety. My predicament was both unenviable and difficult. If I could not remain in Kiev, then I could not resume my former position as superintendent of the factory. Thus deprived of my only source of income, I could not imagine how I would otherwise provide for my family. I had always planned on being able to return to the existence I had previously enjoyed, but now I had to confront a different reality. I had to begin considering the option of moving and starting life anew.

About this time, a committee was formed to help handle my affairs. It was comprised of Dr. Bikhoffsky from Zaitzev's Hospital, Rabbi Aaronson and the noted financier Joseph

Marshak. They took it upon themselves to find a way for me to earn a living elsewhere.

One day, a representative of the *New York American* came to see me. Through an interpreter, he offered me a lucrative proposition. If I would agree to come to America and make appearances across the country for twenty weeks, then he would pay me four thousand dollars. Even though I told him from the very beginning that I wasn't interested, he insisted I take more time to consider his proposal. When he returned for my answer a few days later, he said that, even if I refused now, the offer would always remain open.

"Besides," he advised, "even though you are no longer imprisoned, you must still bear the burden of supporting your family. You may be enjoying your freedom now, but at some point, you will have to concern yourself with earning money. You won't be able to stay in Kiev, and you won't be able to live on other people's sympathies forever. If you come to America, you ought to accept my offer. I will take care of everything. Even if you get a better offer, I'll double it. In the meantime, I want you to sit down and give me a few autobiographical facts."

I did as he asked, and we had a nice conversation for several minutes. Before leaving, he paid me one thousand dollars.

"This," he said, "is for permission to publish your story in our newspaper." He also gave me a personal souvenir, a golden watch. A few days after his departure, I received a telegram from H. Marcus of New York, proposing a three-year contract to work in his banking house. The salary would be ten thousand dollars a year.*

---

* In 1913, these were sizable sums indeed.

I must admit that I found these offers tempting, especially when I considered my situation. I was losing my health, my job and my city of residence. Nevertheless, I respectfully declined.

My committee of guardians also agreed that I should reject this offer, in addition to several others. There was a certain Jewish woman in Paris who wanted to give me a house worth about three-quarters of a million francs, if I would come to Paris with my family. I decided to decline her magnanimous offer. It was going to be difficult enough to relocate to a different country; I refused to have to deal also with a language I could never learn.

Among the many other generous proposals was an offer extended to me by a Mr. Gershovitz, a factory owner from Odessa. His son, who lived in New York and was reputedly worth over a million dollars, had given his father twenty five thousand dollars to settle me and my family in New York. He also offered to establish a trust fund that would provide for all my needs.

I referred Mr. Gershovitz to Dr. Bikhoffsky, who was the chairman of my committee. Dr. Bikhoffsky, however, refused even to entertain the offer, which understandably greatly angered Mr. Gershovitz.

"Am I gaining something from this?" Mr. Gershovitz protested. "I just want to do something nice for Mr. Beilis, as one Jew for another. Why won't you even listen to what I have to say? It doesn't matter to me where Mr. Beilis goes, but wherever it is, he ought to be adequately cared for. I know you want to send him to Palestine. That's fine. Just make sure he'll be able to survive there in comfort and not have to suffer any further privations. If you can't send him to Palestine, why not send him to America where he can live a decent life? If as a result of your advice, Beilis ever finds himself in need, it will be your fault. You will never forgive yourself. His future is in your hands."

But Dr. Bikhoffsky steadfastly refused to reconsider.

Similar proposals came from Berlin, Vienna and London. In London, it was the Rothschild family that wanted to befriend me. They offered to give me a fully furnished home that would become my property as soon as I arrived in London. Mr. Rothschild even dispatched a young Jewish student to help me with the move to England. I was told, however, that the damp climate in London was unsuitable for me. My stint in prison had so adversely affected my health that I was left in a permanently weakened condition.

Somehow, the Kiev press learned of Mr. Rothschild's benevolence. In the same article, the public was also informed that I had decided not to accept this offer either.

CHAPTER 35

To Palestine

While deciding where I should go, I sorely missed having the counsel of Mr. Gruzenberg, my former lawyer. I knew he would be the best one to advise me, for with his experience, he would know what I ought to do and what I should avoid. I felt certain that this man who had been ready to sacrifice everything to save me from prison, would also be willing to help me in any way he could.

Mr. Gruzenberg, however, was out of the country, recuperating from the ordeal of the trial, which had taken a terrible toll on his health. While he was abroad, I had received a letter from him in which he asked what I was doing. He had expressed surprise that I was still in Kiev.

"I have suffered much less than you," he had written, "and yet I feel completely exhausted. You, Mr. Beilis, have suffered much more for even longer, so you must surely be experiencing disturbing repercussions. Why don't you go away somewhere for a rest? I understand your situation quite well. The same thing happened with some of my other clients. After it is all over, people forget about you. I cannot conceive of your remaining in Kiev in such an insecure predicament. Why isn't anyone doing something to help you?"

I heard people discussing my future, but nothing practical seemed to result. I had nothing more tangible than words. Finally, the committee came to an agreement, and it was decided that I ought to be sent to Palestine. Mr. Marshak and Dr. Bikhoffsky were opposed to this plan and had wanted me to settle elsewhere. In the end, Rabbi Aaronson prevailed. Palestine it would be.

Then the committee asked what occupation I would like to choose for myself.

"We'll give you the means to take up whatever new endeavor you would like," they had proffered. "Do not consider it a gift. It is the least we can do for you."

I couldn't decide upon anything specific. They needed an answer that was concrete and definitive, and I was not able to make such a choice.*

"Gentlemen, I cannot make a decision right now," I finally explained to them. "I think it would be better for you to make up

---

* Beilis has attempted to describe the suffering he endured throughout this ordeal, but it is impossible from his account alone for the modern reader to fully comprehend imprisonment and torture in a Russian dungeon, especially during the reign of Czar Nicholas II. It would be reasonable to assume that he was still so physically and emotionally affected that he did not want, or perhaps was not able, to deal with such matters.

my mind for me. I wouldn't be averse to having a little house that would bring in enough income to provide me with a modest means of support. It would also be nice if there were a little land connected to the house. I very much like to farm and always wanted to live on the land."

"In that case," concluded Mr. Marshak, "there is no better place than Palestine. We'll take care of everything."

The plan was for me to first go to Trieste and rest for a month. From there, I would leave for Palestine. I began preparing myself to leave Russia, Holy Russia.

I must confess that it was not easy. There were many people in Russia such as the Black Hundreds who were eager to shed Jewish blood, but on the other hand, there were also many wonderful Russians. Even many Russian prisoners, supposedly depraved criminals, had wept with me in jail. There were countless Russian children who had not slept nights and prayed to God for my release. And what about the Russian intelligentsia? From the beginning, they had taken up my cause, often risking their personal and professional safety on my behalf. How great was the jubilation of these people when their efforts helped bring about my vindication! It was not only the heartwarming visits from hundreds of Christians that made me realize this, but also all the letters and notes that continued to flow in from all over the country.

It would be hard to leave these people, but it was going to be even more difficult to part with my native land, the land where I had been born and raised, where I had lived my life, in anguish and joy.

My departure was to be kept a secret. No one, not even my

relatives, were to know. We had to take these various precautions because my life was still in danger. The day I went to the Governor's palace to get my passport, as soon as I joined the line of about seventy people ahead of me, I was immediately recognized. The person at the head of the line let me have his place, and I went straight into the Governor's office, where I was well received. A chair was brought in and my passport was readied in moments. I was courteously escorted to the cab and bidden a hearty good-bye.

A few days after my visit to the passport office, there were big headlines in the newspapers broadcasting my imminent departure. We had thought that we had been so careful keeping the details of my move secret, but obviously, we had not. We hadn't wanted my enemies to even know that I was leaving, but since the actual day and time of my secret departure was still undisclosed, I felt relatively safe. We selected a day when the crowds would be busy with their vodka. I left in December of 1913.

CHAPTER 36

From Kiev to Trieste

Good-bye, Kiev. Good-bye, Mother Russia. Farewell my native land and all the friends I've lived with my whole life! I am leaving for the land of our fathers, for the Holy Land, where once flowed milk and honey, and which has always been dear to my heart. I am going to rest my body and soul in the Land of Israel. These were the thoughts that occupied my mind.

On the evening I was scheduled to leave, a party was staged by a friend of mine to camouflage my exit. Dr. Bikhoffsky went to the station ahead of me to buy the tickets so I could go directly into the train and be seated at once without being seen. Black Hundreds were prowling everywhere.

I did not even say good-bye to my brother and sister; they hadn't been told I was going.

As a coach drove up to my house in the dark, I put on glasses and a huge cloak so I wouldn't be recognized. My wife and children had left on an earlier train and were waiting for me in Kazatin. From there, we were all to take another train directly to the Austrian border. The manager of Zaitzev's factory, Mr. Dubovik, accompanied us.

We spent the whole night cooped up in the cab as if in a dungeon. We couldn't let anyone see us, for fear of being recognized. At the break of day, I went out into a passageway for a minute.

I noticed two Russians strolling by. The moment they saw me, they came over and asked, "Aren't you Mr. Beilis?" I became very nervous and suspected that these Russians were spies. For all I knew, the Black Hundreds had sent people out to assassinate me. Either way, I had to be careful.

"I wish I were Beilis," I tried to joke. "He's probably in America by now. Do you know him?"

"Oh, yes," one of the men exclaimed. "I was in his house."

When some of the Jewish leaders in Berlin learned of my plans, they sent two men to the Austrian border to facilitate our crossing. These men arrived at the station ahead of us and told the officials whom they were expecting. When we pulled into the border town of Podvolotchisk, two Austrian officials came on board the train to check passports. The instant they saw ours, we were told to proceed. They didn't even check our baggage.

Once we were on the other side of the border, we had to wait a short while for a train to Lemberg. During the interval, a rumor spread through the little town that I was there. Jews came running from all directions, and a great many tears of happiness were shed.

The news of my arrival reached the Jews of Lemberg just before we did. As our train slowly pulled into the station, I looked through the car windows and could hardly believe my eyes. The whole platform, the station house and the adjoining streets were lined with people. The cheering was deafening.

Had the train pulled out immediately, it wouldn't have been so bad. The problem was that there was a brief scheduled layover. The crowd insisted that I come out and show myself. I really didn't want to make a public appearance, but the stationmaster entered my car and begged me to come out, if only for a minute. He seemed to fear that the crowd might somehow damage the station. Besides, a number of people had threatened to stand on the rails and block the train. I had no choice but to go out and address the people. A few minutes later, we were on our way to Vienna.

We reached Vienna in the early hours of the morning. There we were met by Adolph Stern, a Mr. Kaminka and other representatives of the Jewish community. We had tea in the train and were driven to our hotel, where we expected to have a little rest. We were there but a few minutes when there was a knocking at the door.

It was Mr. Stern announcing that some of the foremost Jews of Vienna had come to pay their respects. Mr. Stern engaged an additional suite of rooms as a reception area to accommodate the many people who came to visit me during my stay. That first day brought an assemblage that included professionals, lawyers, professors and doctors. Some of the doctors mentioned they would like to examine me, to make sure I was well. I gave them permission, and they gave me a clean bill of health. They did note that I was suffering from extreme exhaustion, which was understandable considering the circumstances and all I had endured.

A special dinner was arranged for that day and about sixty people were in attendance. Some of the most prominent men in town came, including the editor of the *Neue Freie Presse*, a Viennese newspaper.

Between the official receptions and the barrage of visitors, we were kept busy. I was taken in an automobile for a tour of Vienna, which was a wonderful city with many engaging sights. We drove to the Jewish Musical School, where the cantor sang appropriate chapters from Psalms and the choir enchanted us with a performance.

After two days, it was time to leave and continue south, on to Trieste, where we were to be met by Rabbi Chajes, who would eventually become the Chief Rabbi of Vienna. It was decided that my stay there ought to be kept confidential. Since all the hotels were required to have their guests register their passports, Rabbi Chajes found a special place for me that was willing to waive this stipulation.

We ate our meals in the home of a certain *shochet* who lived in the community. We made it quite clear to our children that my name must not be mentioned. That first Friday night, when we were having Sabbath dinner with the *shochet* and his family, the conversation shifted to the Beilis case. There were about thirty people gathered around the table, and one person reported that Beilis had been in Trieste but was forced to continue his journey incognito so that the Black Hundreds could not find him.

Upon hearing these words, one of my children could not

refrain from bursting out in laughter. Some of the men looked at the child, and one of them asked why she had laughed. Everyone began whispering and exchanging glances. It didn't take long before the entire town knew I was there. Bedlam abounded, and I was besieged with requests for autographs.

In the end, Rabbi Chajes was duly reproached for having kept my whereabouts a secret, and a formal reception was held for me in the ballroom of a big hotel. It seemed like thousands attended. I ended up staying in Trieste for a whole month.

CHAPTER 37

In the Land of Israel

Finally, the day came for us to depart from Trieste and begin our voyage to Israel. We were leaving Europe behind forever and embarking on what I hoped would be the last leg of our journey. Israel would be my home, the place where I expected to spend the remainder of my life in peace.

As soon as we boarded the ship, I was recognized and received a great deal of attention from the other passengers, Jew and gentile alike. One group of Christian passengers presented me with a gift, and the ship's doctor, who had asked for permission to come to my cabin for a visit, showed me my picture which he had clipped out of a magazine.

When we passed through the port of Alexandria, mobs of people who wanted to see me had gathered on the docks. As the ship was entering the port, a number of dignitaries came out in small boats to meet the ship and bid me welcome. I was greeted by a band and representatives from the various Jewish organizations. No sooner had we reached land than I was invited to attend a *bris* being conducted by one of the local Sephardic families. I was really too tired, but excuses were of no avail. At the celebration, I was honored with all sorts of testimonials.

The closer we got to our destination the better I felt. We finally reached Haifa on February 16, 1914. We were home.

A boat was dispatched to carry us ashore. Once we landed, I was met by a great gathering of Jews, including many rabbis. A delegation of Israeli school children carried flags and flowers. The children sang, and a band played.

Arabs were also there in full force, proclaiming, "Long live Beilis!" One of the Arab chiefs, who owned the finest coach and pair of horses in the whole district, honored me by placing his personal coach at my disposal for the drive to Tel Aviv. In the past, this honor had only been extended to such exalted a guest as Mr. Rothschild when he had come to Palestine for a visit. Not satisfied with this munificent gesture, the chieftain himself, accompanied by his attendants, rode at the head of the procession as a sign of respect. All along the route to Tel Aviv, the road was lined with a great many Jews who had come from the colonies especially for this occasion.

Arriving in Tel Aviv, I was taken to the Herzl Hotel, where I was again greeted by representatives of the various local organizations and colonies.

The Land of Israel had an invigorating effect on me, instilling my life with hope. The surroundings, nature, the people, each in its way inspired me with a renewed vigor and the desire to live. When we had left Kiev, it had been cold, and the fields were covered with snow. Here everything was green, and the sun was warm. It was the most beautiful season of the year in Palestine. The hills and the fields were covered with vegetation, and everything was in bloom.

I couldn't get enough of the fresh air. For quite some time, I would wander around the country, inhaling long, deep breaths of the pristine air. At first, I couldn't sleep. Why waste such a fragrant, exhilarating moonlit night on sleep?

A week after my arrival, a deputation of citizens from Jerusalem came to inquire if I planned to settle permanently in Tel Aviv or in Jerusalem. They said it would offend the honor of Jerusalem for me to reside anywhere else.

"Aren't Jaffa and Tel Aviv also a part of Palestine?" I asked.

"Yes, of course," they replied, "but it was the Jews of Jerusalem who prayed for your welfare at the Wailing Wall."

I informed them that I intended to go there in a couple of weeks. I knew they wanted to prepare a reception for me, but I preferred to keep my itinerary private. The many appearances had caused my already weakened condition to deteriorate further. I also feared that the public attention would prevent me from experiencing Jerusalem the way I wanted to.

The truth is, after only two weeks, I was completely drained. My schedule had been even more demanding than immediately following the trial. It was almost the season of the Passover holiday, and this was a time when tourists flocked to Palestine by the thousands. Every ship brought a load of perhaps seven or eight hundred people, all of whom, it seemed, included a visit to me on their itinerary. Thus, in addition to the numerous residents of Palestine, I had to also contend with all these additional people who wanted to see me or shake my hand or in some way express their support and sympathy.

At last, we made our way to Jerusalem. Some of the gentlemen in my party wanted to go along with me. Upon our arrival, we checked into the Amdursky Hotel. My name, however, was not disclosed.

A few hours after our arrival, one man recognized me. The proprietor of the hotel was very much insulted, insisting he should have been let in on the secret, especially since he had set aside a special suite of rooms for me. Within no time, the news spread throughout the town, and the relentless receptions began. In the three days I spent in Jerusalem, I had to visit the synagogues, inspect the hospitals and charity institutions and inscribe my name in countless albums.

For me, the highlight was my visit to the Wailing Wall and the site of the ancient Temple. Approaching the Wailing Wall, I was reminded of the words of the Jerusalem Jews: "We prayed for you at the Wailing Wall."

Jews throughout the world had prayed for me, from the time of my imprisonment until the day of my release. They realized that my tribulations were as much a communal concern as they were a private ordeal. I was being tried not as Mendel Beilis but as a Jew, and as such, every Jew shared my fate.

Standing at the Wailing Wall, I could envision my fellow Jews beseeching God on my behalf just as they had wept and prayed for almost two thousand years bemoaning one tragedy after another, starting with the most devastating tragedy of all, the loss of our Temple. Thus had begun our bitter exile, of which my trial was but one episode. The history of our life in the Diaspora served as a record of our national sorrows. How appropriate it was that prayers for me were offered at this holy, historic site.

With mixed feelings, I caressed the old wall that stood so stoically as a silent witness both to our ancient glories and our modern ignominies. I relived the whole Jewish exile and also re-experienced my own sorrows.

Standing there, absorbed in my own thoughts, I heard a sudden cry. I saw Mr. H. Berlin, one of the members of my party, crying. This surprised me, because he was a man so far removed from his religion that he bore no signs of Jewishness whatsoever. His daughter, who was a doctor and couldn't even speak Yiddish, was also sobbing emotionally.

Mr. Berlin later explained to me that he had cried both from sadness and joy.

"I reminded myself of our exile," he explained. "But I also saw that there is new hope in a Jewish homeland."

From Jerusalem, I returned to Tel Aviv and gradually began the process of becoming a resident. For a month, we remained in the hotel, until we moved in with the Chacham Bashi, the chief Sephardic rabbi.

The welcoming receptions continued until well after Passover, because the steady stream of tourists continued unabated and the local population did not let any opportunity pass without coming up with some way to include me in their various activities. For example, at *Purim* time, hundreds of Jews came to my house to dance and sing. This went on all through the night until the wee hours of the next morning.

As time went on, I became more attached to Palestine. The climate was very good for me and healed my wounds, both physical and spiritual. Within a short time, I felt as though I was a native who had been born in Palestine and lived there all my life. I genuinely enjoyed the country and everything in it, from the people to the inanimate things. It was in Tel Aviv that I learned to appreciate what it meant to be Jewish and live a Jewish way of life. I saw for the first time a race of proud, uncringing Jews, who lived life openly and unafraid.

When people would plead with me to go to America, it was easy to answer them.

"Before, when I was in Russia," I explained, "the word Palestine conjured up a waste and barren land, yet I still chose to come here in preference to any other country. Now that I have come to love the land, I am even more resolved to stay!"

The Jewish education that my children could receive was in and of itself enough of a reason to stay in Palestine. I came with five children, three sons and two daughters. In Russia, I had always lived among Christians, one Jew among four thousand non-Jews, thus it was extremely difficult to raise my children in a Jewish way. They didn't even know Yiddish; to dream of learning Hebrew was ludicrous. It was impossible even to conceive of giving them a full Jewish education.

In Palestine, however, my children had the opportunity of living in an unadulterated Jewish environment and receiving the best Jewish education imaginable.

At last, I thought, I am settled. At last, I can get on with building a new, peaceful life for myself and my family.

Postscript

Once again, Mendel Beilis found himself at the mercy of events beyond his control. Most of the world was either embroiled in World War I or caught up in its aftermath, and Palestine did not prove to be the safe haven Beilis so desperately sought. In 1920, at the age of forty-six, Beilis emigrated to America and settled in New York City, where he lived until his death in 1934.

In New York, Beilis wrote his personal memoirs, *The Story of My Sufferings*, which were published in 1926 by Beilis himself. Originally composed in Yiddish but published in English, the original edition contains two articles written by Beilis's first attorney, Arnold Margolin, in which he pays tribute to those Russian gentiles who valiantly assisted the effort to free Mendel Beilis. There is also a special memorium honoring Rabbi Jacob Mazeh for his extraordinary performance at the trial and his lifelong dedicated service to Russian Jewry. Also of interest at the end of the book is an "Honor List" of individuals and workers' organizations that financed the publication of the book by paying thirty cents for each of twenty-three hundred copies.

This personal memoir provides posterity with a rare inside view of a martyr's ordeal, but it by no means tells the whole story of the Beilis trial, either from the prosecution's side or the defense's. It does, however, form an invaluable addition to the large body of records and literature pertaining to this sensational trial. In addition to the actual stenographic record of the trial, which fills three immense volumes, the archival materials also contain a voluminous collection of articles that appeared in Russian and foreign newspapers. But the most remarkable body of correspondence concerning the Beilis trial was discovered after the Revolution of 1917 in the Czar's secret papers.

It is here that the criminal complicity of the Czar and his officials is factually detailed. Goluboff, Tchaplinsky and Schtcheglovetoff were all conspirators who, with the full knowledge of the Czar, carried out their scheme to make an innocent Mendel Beilis the quintessential scapegoat. These incriminating papers reveal the extent of their involvement in the falsification of documents and testimony. There is included the original medical report, as well as the "altered" versions. Receipts were found for payments to Kossovsky, Zamyslovsky and others for "services" rendered. At the time of the verdict, however, the general public was totally unaware of the government's treachery. Ironically, the verdict of acquittal actually allayed some of the criticism of the Czar, for it showed that the Russian justice system was still capable of freeing an innocent man.

Even after the trial, the governmental agitation did not cease. In an effort to repair the government's image abroad, the Minister of Justice paid a member of the Duma named Zamyslovsky, an original organizer of the trial, seventy-five thousand rubles to publish a work entitled, *The Murder of Andrei Yustchinsky*. Defending the Czar's persecution of the Jews, he wrote, "The fanatic murder committed by the Jews in order to obtain Christian blood is not a legend even in the twentieth century; it is not a blood libel. It is a terrible reality, and many who doubted and hesitated about it became convinced after the Kiev trial."

After the Revolution of 1917, the Provisional Russian Government immediately set about the task of prosecuting former Czarist ministers for crimes against the Russian people. The Beilis case was the first case submitted for investigation. In the summer of 1919, although the archives of the Czar had not yet been researched and the commission was only allowed to investigate illegal acts done in an official capacity, the Moscow Revolutionary Tribunal convicted Minister of Justice Shtchedlovitoff, Ministers of the Interior Makaroff and Maklakoff and Director of Police Bielezky ordered them shot. Zamyslovsky and Shmakoff died in the interim. Prosecutor Viper had died awaiting trial following his indictment in 1919. Vera Tchebiriak was shot in Kiev in 1918.

While this new edition of Beilis's memoirs will undoubtedly stimulate new interest in this dark chapter of history, it will hopefully also correct certain misconceptions about Beilis that may have arisen after the publication of Bernard Malamud's *The Fixer* in 1966. *The Fixer* was a highly acclaimed work of fiction whose plot was contructed around a twentieth century Russian blood libel trial strongly reminiscent of the Beilis trial. The resemblance, however, ends there. Malamud's Yakov Bok was never meant to be a representation of Mendel Beilis. Bok was an obscure little handyman fleeing from his heritage, while Beilis, manager of a huge factory, was not "a little man," and he certainly was not fleeing from his heritage. In an era of rampant assimilation, even in the totally hostile, gentile environs of the factory where he lived and worked, he was conspicuous as "the Jew with the beard." Throughout his memoirs, Beilis proudly and repeatedly portrays himself as a religious Jew. The first words he spoke at his trial were "I am a Jew."

Mendel Beilis was an honorable man, a man of great courage and dignity. Even his accusers confessed that they could find no flaws in his character. His industriousness and integrity were beyond reproof; he had served loyally in the army of the Czar, and he had broken no laws, violated no rules. And above all, the faith and courage he displayed throughout his ordeal was truly remarkable. Had he at any time "confessed" or succumbed to his tormentors, the history of the Jews of Kiev, and perhaps of all Russia, would have contained an additional tragic chapter. Yet Mendel Beilis endured and, in the end, prevailed.

Shari Schwartz
Editor

The Jewish Response

The Beilis Affair shook the ground under those Jews who had thought that the modern world was a more rational one, a world in which outrageous accusations might be levied but would certainly not gain credence. When Mendel Beilis was brought to trial for a blood libel accusation, it seemed that the progress of a century would be completely wiped away in an instant.

Jews around the world were stirred to action. There was also an outpouring of sympathy from non–Jews who recognized the injustice and absurdity of the accusations. A progressive newspaper in Germany reported that "libels that echo with the style and content of the darkest medieval times are being hurled against the Jewish minority in Russia." Diplomats, statesmen and other men of prominence urged the Russian government to retreat from this bizarre enterprise. But against this flood of outrage, the anti-Semites of the world only strengthened and increased their own accusations.

The Jewish world was in turmoil. In congregations around the globe, special daily prayers were instituted for the deliverance of Beilis and all the Jewish people. Community leaders, rabbis, *chassidic rebbes* and influential activists became involved. The Chazon Ish was an active participant in the fight, as were Rabbi Meir Shapiro, the Lubliner Rav, the Lubavitcher Rebbe and the Chortkover Rebbe. The main thrust of their efforts was ambitious. They sought not only to clear Beilis of the unfounded charges but also to uproot the very idea of the blood libel.

The lawyer that headed the defense team was the legendary Oscar Gruzenberg. He knew that the prosecution's attack was going to be directed against the Talmud and other works of Jewish scholarship and that the expertise in devising a defense would have to be provided by the rabbis. Rabbi Mazeh, Chief Rabbi of Moscow, was chosen to head the rabbinic advisory team for the defense.

Prior to the trial, the Chortkover Rebbe invited Rabbi Mazeh for a lengthy discussion of the Beilis case. Rabbi Mazeh records his recollections of these momentous talks in great detail in his memoirs.

The Chortkover Rebbe, speaking to Rabbi Mazeh with great deference, posed the following question: "I have heard that Rabbi Mazeh has been summoned to provide expertise in Torah and in *Halachah* for the Beilis trial. I am aware of his great knowledge and learning, but I cannot help but wonder about his relationship to *chassidus*. I want to point out that if, Heaven forbid, he won't defend *chassidus* with full fervor, they will try to pin the blame on the *chassidim*. But remember that the accusation will not remain behind the courtroom doors, on the outside they will claim that all Jews are *chassidim*."

Rabbi Mazeh responded that he was descended from a *chassidic* family and that he had begun to learn *chassidus* at an early age, both from rabbis and from books. He explained that, in preparation for the trial, he now intended to review them in great depth. He also related that he had been assured by people in Kiev that they would provide him with a list of all the Jewish works the prosecution intended to use in its attack. Beyond that, he assured the Rebbe, "whenever I encounter something difficult, I will turn to the *chassidic* leaders for directions."

The conversation then turned to the actual case. Rabbi Mazeh told the Rebbe that he had just received a copy of one of the arguments to be made by the Catholic priest Pranaitis. He intended to attack a quote from *Midrash Talpios*. The particular quote dealt with a comparison of gentiles to cattle. The *Midrash* went on to say that the Lord had given them the appearance of people out of respect for the Jews, since it was more appropriate for princes to be served by donkeys that seemed human.

"How do you suggest that I explain this *Midrash*?" Rabbi Mazeh then asked the Chortkover Rebbe.

"It is obvious that this quote is correct," the Rebbe replied. "Is it possible that people who do not resemble donkeys would bring an accusation of ritual murder, a blood libel, against a people who refrain from eating an egg if it has even a spot of blood on it? As to what to answer in court, I think you will know what to answer."

They discussed various approaches and the true meaning of

the various quotations. They also discussed difficult passages in *Kabbalah* and concepts of *chassidus*. The Rebbe put his extensive library at the disposal of Rabbi Mazeh; among the books, Rabbi Mazeh found several that he intended to cite as evidence for the defense during the trial. The two men even examined various publications by anti-Semites in order to understand what approach the prosecution would use. The Rebbe then arranged that additional books be provided to Rabbi Mazeh from the library in Vienna. Rabbi Mazeh returned to Moscow via Vienna, confident that the prayers of the Rebbe and his blessings would help him in his important mission.

Mr. Gruzenberg, the chief defense counsel, also turned to the Lubavicher Rebbe for help in preparing his arguments. The Lubavicher Rebbe sent a letter of strong encouragement to Gruzenberg, and Gruzenberg kept this letter in a golden box, evidence of how precious this was to him. The Rebbe also sent Gruzenberg a certificate he had received from Czar Nicholas I designating the Lubavitcher Rebbe as an "honored citizen for all generations." In addition, the Rebbe assigned his brilliant *talmid*, Rabbi Levi Yitzchak, to assist in the preparation of the defense, especially in the area of *Kabbalah*. In all of his numerous letters and directives, the Lubavitcher Rebbe attempted to disprove all these allegations conclusively, to eliminate the very idea of the possibility of a blood libel from the non-Jewish world.

Gruzenberg, in his closing argument, following the instructions of the Rebbe, turned to Bielis and said, "Mendel Beilis! Even if the judges should close their ears and their hearts should turn from the truth and convict you in the law, do not despair. Turn your soul over the Lord. Say, *Shema Yisrael*."

Much later, at the end of the affair, with Beilis acquitted, the Lubavitcher Rebbe wrote a letter expressing his deep fears and sense of foreboding regarding the safety of the Jewish people. He dealt with the issue of the hatred that had been unleashed and the constant incitement of the populace against the Jews. The Beilis affair was over, but the Jewish people were not safe. The era of pogroms and massacres, organized openly or secretly by the government, was not over.

On October 8, 1913, right after *Yom Kippur*, the trial opened. The long-awaited spectacle was now under way. Jew and non-Jew in Russia and around the world awaited the outcome with breathless anticipation.

As the trial began, the indictment accused "Menachem Mendel the son of Tuviah Beilis, 39," of having murdered "together with other people, not discovered, under duress of mysterious religious obligations and rituals, one Andrei Yustchinsky."

The twelve jurors were carefully chosen; their identities and ideologies had been thoroughly prepared prior to the charade of the trial. The first witnesses testified to such blatant lies that the defense lawyer did not even feel compelled to discredit their testimonies. These preliminary stages were clearly a farce, and the audience, near and far, waited for the real trial to begin. At last, the parade of "experts" began. And the trial became an examination of the Talmud's view on various issues.

"What does the Talmud say about the place from which the soul exits the body?"

"Is it correct that the Talmud states that stealing from a gentile is permissible?"

The constant refrain was about the Talmud. There, in the depths of the main courthouse of Kiev, all one could hear was "Talmud." The prosecutor was prepared with an avalanche of quotes from the *Halachic* (legal) and the *Aggadic* (homiletic) portions of the Talmud. Anti-Semites around the world had done their homework and had rallied to the cause of condemning the Jewish people and the Jewish religion in a court of law.

The crucial question was posed: "How dare the Jewish sages claim that [the Jewish people] are called *adam*, man, while the idol worshippers are not called *adam*?"

The illustrious Rabbi Meir Shapiro was then the Rabbi of Galina. (Later, he would establish and serve as the head of the famous *yeshivah* of Lublin, and he would also institute the *Daf Yomi*.) When Rabbi Shapiro heard about attacks against the Talmud, he understood that the Talmud was being accused of inciting Jew against non-Jew. Rabbi Shapiro sent off a very clear letter to Rabbi Mazeh dealing with this accusation. He told him to explain to the court that a very important insight into the nature of the Jewish people is revealed in this Talmudic quote.

"The Torah states," he wrote, "that *kol Yisrael areivim zeh lazeh*, all Jews are responsible for each other. (*Shevuos* 39) According to this principle, it stands to reason that the fate of Mendel Beilis, for example, which is in essence the fate of one single Jew, nevertheless touches the entire Jewish people. The Jewish people tremble for his welfare and would do everything in their power to remove the prisoner's collar from him. What would have been the reaction of the gentile world if one specific gentile had been accused of a similar crime and was standing trial in a faraway country? Clearly, no more than the people of his own town would show any interest in the libel. Perhaps, at most, people in other parts of his own country would criticize the proceedings. But people in other countries? They certainly wouldn't take a personal interest in him.

"This, therefore, is the difference between the Jewish people and all other peoples. The Jews are considered *adam*, the singular form of the word man, an indication of the extreme solidarity of the Jewish people. For us, when one Mendel Beilis is put on trial, the entire Jewish world stands at his side like one man. Not so the other peoples of the world. They may very well be considered *anashim*, the plural form of the word man, but they cannot be considered *adam*, a nation that stands together as a single man."

All the action was not confined to the courtroom. The Chazon Ish became aware that a high official in the government, a close advisor of the Czar, might be willing to listen to an explanation of a Jewish view on shedding blood. The Chazon Ish, who was then still a very young man, wrote an extensive tract, in which he traced the generations from the creation of the world to the time of the Giving of the Torah on Mount Sinai. Clearly and beautifully, he explained the nature of man, the nature of the Jew, the relationship of man and God, how man controls his desires, how he fulfills his role in this world, the role of law and the inherent inferiority of man-made law to the law of the Torah, the importance of education and the intellect of man.

Within this context , the Chazon Ish describes the spiritual fulfillment as man develops his potential by joining his intellect with wisdom. The Talmud, he explained, is a treasure trove of deep and challenging thoughts. Each phrase awes the inquiring mind and cannot be grasped with a superficial reading. He described how Torah leaders devote their lives to the study of the Torah and the Talmud and attempt to plumb its depths. He goes on to state that the "soul" of the Talmud is in its hidden meanings, those that require work and effort. And the only ones who can appreciate the Talmud are those who delve into it.

Several more paragraphs dealt with study, the obligation to study, the enormity of the obligation to study and the great benefits enjoyed by those who engage in this pursuit. He then described the role of the king in Jewish law. In delineating the role of guide to the people, the Chazon Ish was conveying a message about the role of every king.

There is no way of knowing which particular effort of which particular rabbis may have had some impact on the trial. All in all, however, the concerted efforts of the Jews bore out the interpretation of Rabbi Meir Shapiro that "you [the Jewish people] are called *adam*," for the Jews did set aside their internal differences and stood together as "one man" until the verdict of "not guilty" was returned.

Sora F. Bulka
Marcheshvan, 5753 (1992)
Far Rockaway, New York

Beilis (after his acquittal)

Beilis and his family

The cave in which the murdered child was found

Beilis is given
the account
of indictment

Beilis' residence prior to his arrest

The house of Vera Tchebiriak

Beilis leaves street car under guard

The sessions of the Kiev Supreme Court

The Judge, Kiev Supreme Court

P. A. Boldirev

The Prosecuting Attorneys

Chaplinsky

A. I. Vipper, assistant

Witnesses for the Defense

Krassovsky

Brazul-Brushkovsky, journalist

Nakonetchny

Beilis' Counsellors

O. O. Gruzenberg

A. S. Zarudny

W. A. Maklakow

Arnold D. Margolin

B. Karabchevsky

D. G. Grigorovich-Barsky

Experts for the Defense

Rabbi Mazeh

Prof. W. M. Bachterev

Prof. O. O. Kadian

Prof. A. I. Karpinsky

Pavlov, the Czar's surgeon

Prof. I. G. Troyitzki

Experts for the Prosecution

Psichiator Sikorsky

Prof. Kostorotov

Student Golubev

Priest Pranaitis

N. Z. Zamislovsky

Andriusha Yustchinsky's Assassins

M. Latisheff

Vera Tchebiriak

Rudzinsky

Peter Singaevsky

The testimonial presented by the Lydda Yeshiva to
Beilis on the occasion of his acquittal